Heart Gifts

Suzanne M Hurley

A Wings ePress, Inc.
Romance Novel

Wings ePress, Inc.

Edited by: Jeanne Smith
Copy Edited by: April Bennett
Executive Editor: Jeanne Smith
Cover Artist: Trisha FitzGerald-Jung
Images by Pixabay

Wings ePress Books
www.wingsepress.com

Copyright © 2021 by: Suzanne M Hurley
ISBN-13: 978-1-61309-539-3

Published In the United States Of America

Wings ePress Inc.
3000 N. Rock Road
Newton, KS 67114

Dedication

May the joyful spirit of Christmas fill your hearts with love and may Heart Gifts live on forever.

To my mother, who gave every single minute of her life.

To Helen Anderson, who enriches my life with her wisdom, laughter, and serenity.

To John, who shares my love of Christmas lights.

To Mary Lou, who knows all about love and compassion.

To my family, and to Sheila, Theresa, Diane, Dorothy, Marja and Lynda for your constant support.

To my dog, Rico, for being the best companion a girl could have.

To Jeanne Smith, a patient, caring editor who helps bring my words to life. Thank you.

To Trisha Fitzgerald, who designed the cover, and the entire Wings' staff for their dedication and hard work.

* * *

"You are the light of the world. A town built on a hill cannot be hidden. Neither do people light a lamp and put it under a bowl. Instead, they put it on its stand, and it gives light to everyone in the house. In the same way, let your light shine before others, that they may see your good deeds and glorify your Father in heaven."

—Matthew 5:14-16

One

"Cut! Cut!"

Everyone stopped in their tracks.

"Good." Serena Davis nodded to the group. "Thanks for paying attention." She softened her voice, noticing how shocked they looked. Probably because they had never heard her shout. "Now Jacob, you just dropped the baby Jesus for the third time. Is something wrong? Remember, it was *your* idea to have Mary hand you the baby to show how Joseph is a caring dad. Just like your father. *Your* words, not mine. So, what gives?"

"Yeah, I know, but it's just a stupid doll, Ms. Davis." He rolled his eyes. "It's not real."

What have I got myself into? Serena walked over to collect the baby doll, re-attached its head and bundled it up again in a towel, representing swaddling clothes. She shook her head. The first time it hit the floor, a plastic arm had flown off...next, a leg. This last fiasco had the poor thing spinning across the room, crashing into the wall, and losing its head, which had rolled under the piano. One of the shepherds had to crawl around on the floor to retrieve it.

"Yes, you're right," she answered, struggling to remain calm. Showing anger might escalate the situation. She handed the doll back to Jacob. "It may not be real, but on the day of the Christmas pageant, you will be holding an actual baby. I want you to practice showing respect to the doll as if it were a real child. I'm worried you'll drop baby Christopher during the actual performance like you keep letting this doll slip out of your arms. On purpose, it looks to me."

"Yeah, to me, too," Julie said. She was the young girl picked to play Mary and was clearly annoyed, her eyebrows knitted in a frown. "He shouldn't be allowed to hold a real baby, especially my little brother. He's clumsy, always dropping stuff." She glared at him. "And he's annoying."

"Am not." Jacob's face scrunched into a huge scowl.

"Are to," argued Julie, shaking her head in obvious disgust, her long black braids swinging across her face.

"Am not. I can carry around a real baby if I want to. Just not a doll. I don't like dumb, plastic things."

His heated words plus the pained look on his face were extreme... exaggerated, like a caricature. This surprised Serena who had heard his mother talking in the hall the other day about how she had given dolls and trucks to her son when he was little. The goal was to make him tolerant and accepting of both.

If only she could see him now.

Serena also wondered why their former teacher cast the so-called 'class clown' as Joseph. Jacob looked innocent with his mop of red hair and big green eyes. Yet he was well-known throughout the school as someone who would do anything for a laugh. Continually dropping the doll earned him lots of giggles and attention, and fit right in with his usual way of joking around.

Wait a second. She leaned forward. He looked ready to cry. Was something else going on?

Was it possible he was being teased about holding a doll?

Come to think of it, when she'd entered the classroom the other day, she thought she overheard someone say, "*Ja*-cob, *Ja*-cob. Next you'll be wearing *make*-up." She wasn't one hundred percent sure, and she had no idea who said it, but she vowed to keep a closer eye on things in case he was being bullied.

The dropping of the doll had to stop, though. It interfered with their practice, made the other students snicker, and created a mockery of their re-enactment of the Christmas story. Usually, she'd reprimand someone in private, but the third drop had gotten to her. It was just becoming ridiculous and the three shepherds were still bent over laughing at the sight of the doll constantly flying across the room.

"The doll isn't stupid. You're the one's who's stupid," Julie shouted, stamping her foot, pulling Serena out of her thoughts. "The baby Jesus is my little brother, and I don't want you hurting him."

"I won't."

"You will. And he can't be bouncing off the wall either."

More giggling from the cast.

"Okay, everyone. That's enough," Serena said in her sternest voice.

My goodness, they were all middle schoolers acting like children, bickering back and forth, being silly, horsing around. Guess she expected more, especially since she had always been a solemn kind of student herself. She glanced at her watch, her fingers crossed, hoping they were near the end of their rehearsal time.

Good. Saved by time, or lack of it.

"Okay, that's it for today," she called out. "I'd like everyone to gather around me for a moment."

They did, albeit in slow motion, eyes averting, guilt written on their faces. Some bracing themselves for a big lecture on their behavior.

Her eyes raised to the heavens. *Please, God, help me to inspire them, as well as find the words to keep them motivated and give them hope.*

"Great job everyone," she burst out. "This is shaping up well." She smiled at their surprised faces, for of course, the drama they were re-creating was a complete disaster. But she couldn't dwell on that. She had to remain positive. It seemed like the only thing to do in situations like this. If she didn't, it could get worse.

"But we're awful, Ms. Davis," Jake said. He was the innkeeper who had spent most of the rehearsal staring at Lydia, a shepherd. From the looks of it, he was smitten.

"We're like the blooper version of the nativity scene," Julie agreed. "Bet we could get millions of hits on YouTube and go viral."

Everyone nodded their agreement.

Serena groaned. That was all she needed. To be filmed and shown to the world as a failure. How horrifying.

"You're not awful," Serena said, jumping in, attempting to sound confidant. Julie and Jake were right, but Serena didn't want them to know she felt the same. "We just have to practice more. I'm convinced this will be the best Christmas re-enactment yet."

Staring at their skeptical faces, she struggled to hang onto her own optimism. Not easy to do when a lot centered on this pageant. In fact, her whole life.

It has to be good. It just has to. There is no room for error. None whatsoever.

"So same time tomorrow. Let's try something different and perform with costumes. Maybe that will help get everyone in the mood. Oh, and one more thing...and this is very important." She paused for effect, then spoke slowly, emphasizing every word. "Please, no name-calling or fighting allowed. I will not tolerate anyone hurting someone else needlessly. I'm asking you to be kind and caring towards one another and also, to that doll." She watched Jacob roll his eyes for the second time and Julie looked a tad embarrassed. "Remember, this is all about the baby Jesus and the true Christmas story. We must never lose sight of that." She smiled. "So, thanks for coming and have a safe trip home. It might be a bit slippery out there with all the snow, so be careful where you walk. Jacob, may I speak to you for a moment?"

She had made a decision.

"Oh, okay."

She led him to the other side of the room where it was private.

"Am I in trouble?" he asked, as he backed away, eyes widened in fear. "Please don't yell at me or tell my parents. I promise I'll do better."

Serena smiled. "I know you will. I'm just wondering if you are being teased or bullied for taking on the part of Joseph."

As well as keeping an eye out, she decided to ask him directly.

"No, Ms. Davis. I'm not."

Was he telling the truth? She wasn't convinced, as she watched his eyes slide off to the left. He was either embarrassed at his behavior or being mocked.

"Okay, then. You'd tell me if you were, right?"

"Um, guess so."

"I hope you will. Well, see you tomorrow, then." She didn't want to make a big deal out of this, just plant a seed, in case he was experiencing some form of harassment. Opening a door, so to speak.

"Okay, see you."

He ran off to join the shepherds, angels, and all the other students who were busy dragging on their coats and boots. As they headed toward the exit, enthusiastic chatter and laughter following their steps, they brought a smile to Serena's face. Individually, they seemed sweet. Collectively they were a challenge she had to conquer.

The door opened and she could see the snow swirling around in the wind. She'd better get going herself.

She scanned the room, checking to see if it was empty.

Wait! What was going on over there?

She could hear Julie calling Jacob over.

Serena edged closer. She hoped they weren't fighting again.

Julie surprised her. "Sorry for calling you stupid."

"Um, okay. Sorry too for saying the doll is dumb and dropping it. Don't worry. I'll take good care of your baby brother when we perform."

"Thanks." Julie reached over and high-fived him.

Such a sweet gesture, proving miracles really could happen.

After all, Julie was worried about her brother and Jacob wasn't crazy about dolls. It was wonderful to see them call a truce and make peace. Well done.

Julie turned, saw her and winked. Serena mouthed 'thank you,' and they finally left, the last two out the door. Ignoring the fact she should go home as well, she headed to the nearest chair and sat, leaning over, head in hands.

A question tumbled about in her mind.

How was she ever going to pull this hot mess together?

Two

It had all sounded so easy.

"The teacher you are temporarily replacing had the class write the script, cast the Christmas pageant, and everyone knows their part. Your job is simply to hold rehearsals and make sure they will be ready for their big night," Mr. Lemire had said. He was the principal of Angel Christian Elementary School.

Yes, the school really was named Angel, after the town, Angel, Pennsylvania, founded by the late Samuel Angel, a very real person.

"No problem," she'd responded. *"I'm happy to take over directing the play as well as teaching the class."*

Piece of cake, she'd actually thought, figuring the hard work was done concerning the pageant. All she had to do was concentrate on preparing materials and instruction for each subject. The rehearsals would just fall into place.

Except it wasn't easy. Not even close. At least the pageant part of the job.

This rehearsal showed how far they were from being ready. No one took it seriously, no one remembered their lines or knew their moves. What was even worse, no one seemed to care. They were excited about Christmas break, leaving for vacation, getting presents on Christmas Day and that was pretty much it. The pageant was just something they had to endure.

"Excuse, Ms. Davis. Are you all right?"

Startled, Serena looked up to find Principal Lemire standing in front of her. She jumped up fast, knocking her chair over, her face flush at his unexpected arrival.

Angel Christian Church was located right next door to the school. They had been practicing there because it was where the pageant was held each year. The church had a large auditorium in the basement, equipped with a spacious stage, and a lot of room to recreate the Christmas story. It had never occurred to her he'd pop by. It should have, for he appeared to be curious, and had even come in the back door. Was he sneaking in? Spying? Would he do that?

Thank heavens, he'd missed the rehearsal, or she'd probably be fired on the spot for the chaos that had ensued. Picking up the chair, she stopped herself from giggling, picturing him saying in his very proper voice, "Dropping the baby Jesus is not in the script, Ms. Davis."

Wait a second. He'd asked her a question.

"Yes, I'm fine. Just resting my eyes for a minute." She managed to summon up fake confidence in her voice, as well as a smile. No way would she let on she had a catastrophe on her hands.

"Well, the Christmas pageant is in three weeks. How is it going? Good, I presume?"

He might be smiling, but she could see worry in his eyes. Probably because she looked frazzled as opposed to someone in complete control. She reached up to tuck stray hairs back behind her ears and check to make sure her ponytail was intact.

Please, God. Please let me be ready.

"Oh, most certainly."

Don't show your terror. Ever. When in doubt, continue to speak with authority.

Her principal didn't need to know that so far, the play looked like a parade of comics racing through scenes. It was her secret, for now. Her secret and her students', and hopefully they'd keep it quiet.

"Good. Sorry I missed the rehearsal. As I mentioned before, this is very important, for I am adamant that we keep Jesus in Christmas." His shaky smile disappeared, and he now looked dead serious. "I'm looking forward to this. It's the highlight of the year."

The highlight? Of the year? Really?

Great, just great. No pressure, but it looked like a big letdown would be in store if Serena couldn't pull it together.

"You went to school here yourself, didn't you?" he asked.

"Yes, I did."

"You must remember your own Christmas drama?"

Serena nodded but said nothing. No way did she want to think of her pageant, let alone talk about it. It was a bad memory she had stored away. In fact, it was also a total disaster, and saying something about it might invite questions she'd rather not answer.

Eyebrows raised, seemingly noting her silence, he continued, "Well, carry on, Ms. Davis. I look forward to seeing this. Every single parent has responded with a yes to attending that night. It's the best response we've ever received."

Serena continued to smile, even though she wanted to cry. Everyone in town would witness her failure. Bet they were coming because they'd heard from their kids how awful it was and wanted to witness the train wreck first-hand. She just hoped she wasn't shamed out of town. Maybe she should keep her car running that night, as well as a packed suitcase in the trunk, in case she had to make a fast getaway. She could swing by, pick up her dog, and head out of town. Of course, she was kidding, but it could very well be a viable plan B.

Realizing Principal Lemire expected a response, she quickly responded, "Oh, that's wonderful. So exciting." She gushed and it sounded fake, but it was all she could think of to say.

Once more he raised his eyebrows. "Yes, it is. So, carry on."

Watching him walk away, she wondered for about the fiftieth time, how she could pull this off. He seemed to be expecting big things. Huge. Miraculous, even.

Couldn't blame him.

It was a tradition at Angel to have the seventh-grade class re-enact the Christmas story just before everyone left for the holidays. She had never considered it to be the highlight of the year, or how much stock the principal put on it.

Panicking, she started to hyperventilate, sitting back down on the chair. The highlight? And everyone planned to attend?

Oh, no.

Breathe.

In and out. In and out.

Eventually she felt calmer, even though her mind still raced.

The pressure was on, for she needed this to go well.

"This position is temporary, but we are looking for a full-time teacher in the new year," Lemire had added at the interview. *"You never know, you might be the perfect candidate for the job."*

She was counting on it, hoping for it, desperately needing it.

The only reason Serena had been hired for this temporary job was because the current teacher had hurt her ankle while playing basketball. She had to take time off to recover and they needed someone in a hurry. Serena was available and able to take the position fast. In other words, she'd lucked out. Well, the teacher who was hurt hadn't been so lucky, but Serena was relieved she'd gotten the job. Unfortunately, after this rehearsal, her prospects for a future hiring looked bleak. Maybe the pageant failure wouldn't impact the decision?

Who was she trying to kid?

Of course, it would.

Breathe. In and out. In and out.

Don't think about this.

Unfortunately, it was all she could think of.

She had to face the fact there was an even bigger problem than a poor re-enactment of Christ's birth.

She had no singer. No one to deliver the evening's showstopper, "O Holy Night." This carol was the real clincher to making the play a success, for it was a beautiful musical interlude for viewers to reflect on the miracle and beauty of Jesus' birth.

As per tradition, first there was the drama, then a meditation written and delivered by a student, next the song, finally a collection. The donations raised went to someone or several people who needed help in the community. It was engraved in stone here at Angel, a terrific heart-warming event, but overwhelming at the moment.

Apparently, a student by the name of Valerie was the intended singer until her parents pulled her out of school to attend a family reunion in Florida. So far no one in the class wanted to sing the Christmas hymn, no matter how many times she'd begged. Couldn't blame them. It was a tough song with plenty of high notes. Definitely not easy.

Perhaps she could buck tradition and try another song in a lower key that was easier to sing. Probably not. She didn't even want to ask. It would show weakness at a time when she needed to show strength.

She was in way over her head, both in her professional and personal life. All she knew was that she had to pull it off.

Or her mother would lose her beloved bakery.

Her passion, her love, her life.

Three

Howling winds and snow swirling around outside exacerbated Serena's stress. She sighed as she pulled on her coat, slid on her boots and picked up her briefcase. Time to stop worrying and get home to help her mother before the storm heightened as predicted.

Wrapping her scarf tightly around her neck, she trod through the snow back to her classroom to pick up books she needed for tomorrow's lessons. History and geography would be on her agenda tonight, along with baking cinnamon buns.

Gathering everything she needed and stuffing it in a large bookbag, she walked down the hall, wondering if the roads were clear and at least driveable. Snow was pretty to look at, but not so much when manoeuvring a car through ice and slush.

Wait a second.

She stopped in her tracks.

Was someone singing?

And of all things, "O Holy Night?"

Or was it her imagination, spurred on by extreme anxiety over finding a singer?

Where was it coming from?

She swung around.

Aha!

It emerged from the other hallway, a place usually deserted at the end of the day.

Did someone leave a radio on? An iPod? A student from the play perhaps? She sneaked around the corner and was surprised to see a young girl standing there, tall, with long blonde hair, head raised, staring out the window, singing her heart out. Wearing a white ski jacket and a golden knit hat, she looked like an angel.

When she turned her head slightly, Serena recognized her as one of her students, in fact the newest one. Jade was her name, and apparently she had arrived at the school the day before their teacher had ended up in the hospital. She seemed sweet but quiet at rehearsal, having a small part as one of the angels who led the procession down the aisle.

She sings?

Serena hung back, waiting to see if she could hit the high note. Not that she wanted perfection, but a somewhat reasonable attempt would be lovely.

Jade did. Effortless and clear. Right on key, as well.

Tears escaped Serena's eyes at her beautiful tone. With no accompaniment, completely *a cappella*, framed by flakes of snow drifting in the background outside, she was blown away. The girl's voice stunned.

When the last note softly dwindled away, Serena clapped. She couldn't help herself.

Jade turned around, her eyes registering shock, her mouth open in a wide 'O.'

"That was beautiful." Serena took a few steps closer, then hesitated. "You have an amazing voice."

"Um, er, not really."

"Yes, really. I had no idea you could sing like that."

Despite Jade's obvious shyness and self-deprecation, Serena noted her eyes lit up.

"It's my mom's favorite." There was sorrow in Jade's expression as she lowered her gaze. "The rehearsal reminded me of her."

"I love this song, too. And you sing it well."

"Nah. Mom did, though."

Did?

Serena made a mental note to check out this girl's file, for she knew nothing about her. She'd read every student's history, but Jade's hadn't arrived at the school yet, seeing as she was new. Should be soon, though. If not, she'd make a push to get it. It sounded like there was a story here or at least something she should know. She hesitated to ask the girl until she had more facts.

"Have you ever performed at an assembly? I'm looking for an angel, you know, to sing that exact carol."

"Yes, I know, but I'm already an angel in the play."

"But I need a singer. You'd be perfect for the role."

The girl's face closed down. It was like watching a book figuratively snap shut right in front of her.

"Sorry," Jade said softly. "But I just can't do it."

Was she nervous? Serena could understand that. But with a little practice... "Are you sure? Would you like to at least try? I'll help you."

"No."

The girl had a quiet voice. Serena hoped she'd heard wrong. "Pardon?"

"I said, no."

Okay, that was loud and clear.

Calm down, Serena. Don't push. Don't sound so desperate.

Unfortunately, she was. Yes, she was that desperate.

"Well, why don't you think about it? Everyone would be thrilled to hear your wonderful voice."

"Do you think so?" A faint smile tugged at the girl's lips. As if she genuinely wanted to sing.

"Yes, I do." Serena smiled back.

"Er, well, no, I can't."

Silence. She'd shut down again. So odd. Especially with a voice so lovely.

Serena wished she could do something to put that glow of excitement back in the young girl's eyes. Or at least take away the sad, empty look.

No such luck. Jade seemed about to cry.

"Well, okay. I'm sorry for pushing. Do you need a ride home?"

"No, my dad is picking me up."

As if on cue, a male voice called out behind her, "I'm here. Sorry, I'm late. Couldn't find a spot out front like we'd agreed on due to the snow, so I parked in the visitors' section. Figured I'd come in and find you."

Serena turned to see who was talking and watched a man rush down the hall towards them. He was tall, lean, dressed in a parka and jeans, with brown hair on the longish side, cowboy hat perched on top. What struck her were his blue eyes that seemed to pierce right through to the soul. She knew only one other person who had those same eyes.

Oh no.

Her heart raced.

It couldn't be.

She squinted, scanning his face.

It was him.

Matt Jenkins, the one person she detested in the whole world, stood right in front of her, looking handsomer, if that were at all possible.

He was Jade's father?

Four

The woman beside his daughter looked familiar.

Matt studied her face.

She resembled someone he knew.

But it couldn't be her.

Could it?

He'd heard she'd gone away to school and lived in Boston.

It sure looked like her.

He eyed the familiar mass of shiny auburn hair, the slim build, but what drew him was that head tilt thing she did whenever she was startled, nervous or challenged. He'd seen it too many times directed at him and occasionally it still haunted his dreams.

After all, she had been his very first crush.

Was he hallucinating?

Matt couldn't help but just keep staring at her. Sure...yet unsure.

He had to know.

"Serena? Serena Davis?" he stammered out. "Is it really you? Serena the ballerina?"

The head tilt thing just became more pronounced.

"Yes, it's me, but please, no more ballerina nicknames. I heard it every single day at school and thought it'd been buried."

"Oh, sorry." Amazingly he'd managed to anger her in a split second, just like the old days. She'd tried to temper it with a weak smile, probably because his daughter was there, but she was annoyed. In a big way.

Get it together, he thought.

"You two know each other?" Jade's eyes widened in surprise.

"We went to school together."

"And you are Jade's father?" Serena's eyebrows rose, as if she couldn't process this new piece of information.

"Yes, he is," Jade said. "He's here to pick me up."

He watched as Serena glanced back and forth between them, clicking the pieces together. He turned his attention to his daughter, noting the melancholy that hung over her like a dark cloud. It had been there a lot lately, haunting him.

"Was today any better, honey?" he asked.

Jade shrugged.

"No?" He wrapped his arm around her. "It'll improve in time."

"Promise?"

"Promise." Using his other arm, he crossed his fingers behind his back.

It'd been tough pulling Jade out of school in Charlotte. She'd grown up there and all of her friends lived nearby. He'd had no choice. He had to do it. To save them both.

"Is something wrong, Jade?" Serena asked, in a gentle tone of voice.

His daughter shrugged again.

"I'm her teacher, Mr. Jenkins. Did something happen?"

She was the teacher? Her eyes were wide, concerned, and his heart twitched.

Serena was one of the kindest people he had ever met. She always helped anyone in need, and he had even watched her carry spiders out of the classroom, setting them free outdoors. He used to tease her about that but deep down, he couldn't help but admire her. Once he even took part in one of her acts of kindness by helping her deliver cold drinks to construction workers on a hot day.

She taught his daughter?

He had met the regular one at an appointment when they'd first moved to Angel. Jade had informed him they now had a supply teacher, but he never clued in that Ms. Davis was Serena.

He had often thought of her, but figured he'd never see her again.

"Mr. Jenkins, Jade, please. Is something wrong? You're not acknowledging my question, but you seem concerned."

Matt knew Jade wouldn't rat anyone out. However, his need to protect her pushed him. "From what I gather, my daughter is not being accepted by the rest of the class. She's even heard them make rude remarks about her, not even trying to stay quiet about it."

Jade jerked her head back, giving him a dirty look. She felt telling on other students would just make it worse, but he couldn't help it. He needed it to stop. He wanted his daughter to be happy and enjoy school. She'd been through so much these past couple of years and being bullied was not something she could or should have to handle. It had to end and soon.

"I'm okay, really I'm okay," Jade said, loudly.

He knew Serena was watching their interplay. She said softly, "We can talk about it tomorrow, Jade, if you'd like. And don't worry, I won't take any action unless you okay it."

Leave it to Serena to get a handle on things fast and figure out a strategy.

"All right." She gave Serena a relieved smile.

"By the way, your daughter has a lovely singing voice."

"Yes, she does."

Matt felt himself close up. He couldn't help it. Gut instinct took hold. Discussing his daughter's voice was not something he wanted to do. *Ever* again.

"I'm looking for an angel to sing in the pageant. She'd be perfect for the role."

"Oh, I don't think she wants to do that, right, honey?"

"No, Daddy. I don't."

He felt relieved.

"But it's a shame to keep such a beautiful voice hidden," Serena continued.

She sounded desperate. Matt wondered why, but had no time to figure it out or even to care. He had to end this conversation fast. It was too painful.

"It's not your decision to make," he snapped. Judging by how shocked Serena looked, he was being too harsh, but he needed to get off this topic fast. "Sorry, it's just not going to happen."

"Well," Serena said. "Okay, then."

"So, it really is you, Serena Davis. And you're in charge of the Christmas pageant? Do you remember ours?" Now he was the desperate one, trying to change the direction of the conversation.

"Must you bring that up?"

He was surprised by her reaction. She sounded annoyed, for the second time.

"You're not still upset over that assembly."

"Still am."

"What happened, Dad?"

"Oh, nothing," Serena said quickly, too quickly. "Sorry I sounded upset."

"Yeah, it really was nothing," Matt said, noticing the curiosity on Jade's face and regretting he'd mentioned it. In his effort to switch to another topic, he'd summoned up a minefield.

"What are you doing here in Angel?" Serena asked. "I thought you were some busy lawyer in North Carolina."

"I live here now. And you? I thought you were teaching or going to school or doing something in Boston."

"Well, I was. But I'm back home now."

He had no idea she'd be here when he'd moved, and he wasn't sure he liked the idea. Judging by his racing heart, she still had quite an effect on him. An effect he didn't need nor want.

"Dad. Ms. Davis. Sorry to be rude, but can we go now? I have to take care of Gabrielle."

"You're right, honey. We need to go." He looked at Serena. "Gabrielle is her new horse."

"Oh, I understand. I'm a huge animal lover, too. See you tomorrow, Jade."

Somehow, he felt both relieved to get away but surprisingly sad to leave Serena. Even though many years ago they had left on disastrous terms, he still admired her. He'd hoped she'd forgotten about it, but she obviously hadn't. He'd also cared for her back then. Amazingly, she still looked the same and he could feel his face flush, just like it used to do back in elementary school. His schoolboy crush, long dormant, erupted, and he felt like a kid again just wanting to please her.

Guilt surfaced.

He had to get away.

His wife, Maya, had only been gone a little over a year and a half. No way should he be noticing another woman. Even an old love, or crush to be more truthful.

"Come on, Jade. Let's go."

Okay, he sounded brusque. Even rude. But he'd suddenly felt the collar of his coat tighten, suffocating him and he had to leave.

Fast.

Before he somehow made a fool of himself.

Again.

Five

Serena opened the door from her apartment that led into Petals, her mom's bakery/cafe. It swung shut behind her as she took a few steps, stopped, and stood there, relishing the moment.

Closing her eyes, she sucked in big, deep breaths and let them out slowly, savoring the mouth-watering wafts of gingerbread, apple cider, chocolate, vanilla and freshly baked bread.

"Ah, bliss," she whispered to herself.

After getting her fix, she looked around, reveling in the familiarity of what had been her home for twenty plus years. The scattering of tables was decked out in red gingham, each one highlighting a vase of cut red roses, her mother's favorite flower, hence the name Petals. It was once called Rose Petals but eventually shortened.

It was a place of instant solace to the heart.

The room beckoned you to rest a while, enjoy the moment, and calm your mind. The counter displayed an assortment of baked goods to entice the senses, the coffee pot was filled to the brim, and hot chocolate sprinkled with crushed candy canes sat waiting. All around the room was a mixture of nutcrackers of all sizes, shapes and colors, amid red and gold ornaments. Christmas shouted at you here at Petals and invited you to join in its festivity. It was a place of joy. A slice of heaven carved out to delight your senses. It really was the nucleus of Angel. Of course, she was biased, but then again, maybe not.

Many people declare Disney World to be the happiest place on earth, but to Serena, it was right here. Delightful moments were embedded in the charming café nestled in this little town, whose warmth felt like the best hug you ever had. It helped that there was a life-size angel honoring their founder in the town square just outside the door. According to town legend, kind and compassionate Samuel was in love with Christmas and the statue was a constant reminder to go all out to celebrate this special season. In fact, town residents put on a huge push to keep this special holiday in the forefront all three hundred and sixty-five days, and somehow managed to outdo themselves every year. It was not unusual to see Christmas lights sparkling in the middle of July, or candy canes hanging on outdoor trees in August, and the delicious aroma of chocolate permeated the whole town, no matter what month it was.

She loved it here. At times she felt it was inconceivable she'd ever left.

"Good morning, honey," her mother shouted, peeking out from the kitchen door, probably checking to see if any more customers had arrived. Usually a bell rang out when someone new entered, but often it got lost in excited conversation and oven buzzers signaling baked goods were ready.

"Hey, Mom, sure smells good in here."

"I know." She grinned. "You say that every day. Pretty much verbatim."

"And I mean it."

"I know that too, dear."

Her mom hobbled towards her, cane in one hand, the other reaching out for a hug. Serena clasped her tightly.

"Should you be walking around so much, Mom?" she whispered, not wanting to let her go. Ever since her mother had broken her leg,

Serena found herself wishing she could hold her in her arms all day long, keeping her safe and wanting for nothing.

"Yes, my doctor okayed it. Now, go grab a seat. I have a cinnamon bun piled high with icing ready, heated, buttered, just the way you like it."

"I'd rather help you in the kitchen."

"No, no. You did enough last night, preparing lesson plans, then staying up late to help me bake. Time for you to sample the results. Now, sit."

Knowing she wouldn't take no for an answer, Serena sat, mouth-watering at the size of the bun her mom retrieved from a hot plate behind the counter.

Her mother.

Mary Catherine Davis. Barely five feet tall, with shoulder length blonde hair tucked into a hairnet, effervescent, and the sweetest mom a girl could have.

Oh, how she loved her.

Serena's father had died when she was five and they'd arrived here when she was eight. Her grandmother, an outstanding baker, had moved in to help those three years, and taught the two of them all her tips and tricks. When the bakery came up for sale, her mom grabbed it. Serena had grown up here, did her homework at the table in the corner, and helped whenever she could. She especially enjoyed decorating cookies, mirroring her grandmother's creative touch she'd watched all those years. It was her second home, her first being the lovely, spacious apartment above the store. Her mother still lived there while Serena resided in the smaller one in the same building.

"Is something wrong?" Mary asked, setting the plate down.

"Oh, no, not at all." Serena shook her head, pulling herself out of her trove of memories.

"But you usually just dive right in with a cinnamon roll, eating it in seconds."

"Just letting it cool." Serena took her first bite. "Mmmmm..."

"I'll be back with coffee."

"Mom, I don't want you waiting on me. I can get it myself."

She'd already disappeared into the kitchen, amazing Serena at how fast she could move with that cane. It hadn't slowed her down one bit. She probably had gone to retrieve the special Santa mug Serena used every day during the season. It used to be her father's cup, and she treasured it dearly. She'd made sure she knew exactly where she'd packed it when she brought her belongings home with her.

Sigh.

They fought about her mother still wanting to wait on her like a little child, but Mary claimed she loved doing so and wouldn't let her help. At least, when it came to breakfast. Other times she was not so strict. It was a rule that she was to eat something every single morning, hungry or not. Usually, she served up a healthy portion of oatmeal with fruit, but relaxed during the Christmas season. She'd be aghast to know her daughter often skipped breakfast when she was off at school and lived on take-out coffee and muffins during break times.

The kitchen door popped open and out walked Helen Farstein carrying a platter of freshly baked brownies. She was tall, lean, older than Mary, with an energy level that could run circles around most people her age. Serena smiled at her and was rewarded with a grin, as she poured coffee for a new customer who had walked in and was seated at the counter.

Helen had been the first person her mother had hired and had been with them for almost the whole twenty plus years. She was a rock, a hard worker, good listener, and loved to bake, almost as much as her mother.

She had also sent Serena a letter a month earlier which had shocked her to the core.

Dear Serena,

You need to come home and have a long talk with your mother. I'm sure you don't know, but she broke her leg tripping over the back step while taking out the garbage. We've been operating the bakery with fewer hours, bringing in little money. Also, you need to know that Mr. Anderson, who owns the building, is selling the place and has owners in mind. He offered it to your mother, but she can't afford it. If the interested people buy it, it has been made clear that the bakery will be done, finished. Your mother needs your help and won't ask for it. I've suggested she call you, but she doesn't want to bother you. I took the liberty to reach out myself. I know how much you love your mom and how close you are to her and I feel you need to know.

Love, Helen

Serena had sat down fast that day. Either that or fall down. She couldn't even begin to imagine losing the bakery, her mother's pride and joy, basically her whole life. Surely her mom would have told her if there were problems.

Wouldn't she?

Especially the fact she'd broken her leg?

That was huge.

Immediately calling her supervisor at school and explaining she had an emergency, she drove home that day, and was alarmed to see the for-sale sign in front of the building. Everything in the letter was true. Of course, it was not as if Helen ever lied, but Serena didn't want to believe the facts and was shocked her mother had kept silent about her problems. She still recalled that first day back when she'd rolled up her sleeves and worked with Helen all evening so the bakery could open the next day during their normal hours. Serena was committed to staying and helping. No way would she allow her mother to face this crisis alone. They had been a team all her life, more friends than mother/daughter and they were in this together.

There were even more shocks in store.

After scouring the books, she'd also discovered how tight her mom's finances were. She operated in the red. Multiple appliance breakdowns over the years, having to re-do the kitchen to keep up to professional par, less operating hours due to Mary's broken leg equalled a rapidly dwindling income. Not to mention, her mother insisting she help with Serena's school bills, letting on she had more than she did. Amid all of this, once again Helen was right...Mr. Anderson was planning on selling the building to new owners who had other plans and wanted the bakery gone.

She had to help.

After all the years of her mother helping her, it was payback time.

She watched her mom come sailing through the door leading to the kitchen, holding the Santa mug, smiling and greeting a customer with such contentment on her face. It was her dream, and one she'd worked hard to turn into reality. She was the happiest with an apron wrapped around her waist, dots of flour on her face, baking and serving others in her own loving way. She was also a listening ear to everyone, consoling when needed, sharing in the happy times.

Serena was determined.

Somehow, she had to save this bakery.

For her mother.

It was going to happen, no matter what obstacle stood in the way. She had to do it. Her love for her mother drove her, and she was determined to buy this building and secure their future forever.

Of course, her mother argued with her to go back to school, but she took a leave of absence from her doctorate. She had some money saved, but it wasn't enough. They would need a lot more for a down payment and to keep paying a hefty mortgage. When the job at the school opened up, Serena jumped at it. Although the position was temporary, she had a greater chance of getting a mortgage if the school hired her full time. She kept on helping at the bakery as her mother grew stronger, but she needed that teaching job and to be kept on permanently with a steady paycheck. It would make all the difference.

In other words, the Christmas pageant had to be perfect.

If it were, Principal Lemire might put her at the head of the line of applicants. She was convinced of it. Or at least she hoped so.

Serena shuddered at just how bad that rehearsal was. It still shook her.

She had to make it work, though. Somehow.

"Here, dear," her mom said, arriving at the table.

She jumped up to help her.

"Don't worry, I can do this." She placed the mug down on the table.

"I do worry, though," Serena said, sitting again.

"I know. But my doctor said I can move around as much as I want with the cane. I'm almost healed. I've been doing my exercises faithfully and I'm in no pain whatsoever. I'll probably end up stronger than ever."

"Well, that's good news. Can you join me for a few minutes?"

"I'd love to." Mary hurried off to grab a coffee for herself and came back before Serena even had time to object. Stifling her frustration, Serena took another bite of the bun, sighing with pleasure at how good it tasted.

"Granny's cinnamon roll recipe is the best ever," she said. "I'll never get over how it melts in the mouth."

"She definitely was a good cook. I learned from a pro."

Unfortunately, her grandmother had passed away before they'd moved, finally succumbing to cancer. Otherwise, she'd be working away in the kitchen, too.

"Well, you are just as good." Serena looked around. "She would have loved this bakery."

"I was glad that at least we were able to show her photos when we first put a bid in to buy it."

"Which she loved."

"Yes, she did." Her mother smiled.

A sudden burst of barking broke into their thoughts.

"Oh, there goes Holly," Serena said. "I take it she's out romping with Gloria?"

Her mom grinned. "Yes, she is. She whimpered at the door so I let her out. Hope you don't mind. Right now, they're hanging in the back room playing tug games. Or something like that."

"Oh, I don't mind a bit. I figured they were together, since there were no loud barks or face licking to wake me up."

One good thing about living so close to her mother was their two dogs had formed quite the team and were instant companions. Serena had worried about Holly being alone when she was at school, even though she walked her morning, noon and night. Here she had the companionship of another fur friend. Usually whoever was up first let the other dog out as well. Normally, it was her mother, who loved the serenity of working away in her kitchen baking in the wee hours of the morning.

"Well, it still amazes me how my golden retriever and your Havanese dog are best friends."

"I know. Quite sweet actually. Usually Holly is afraid of big dogs, but not yours."

"They're good company for each other." Her mother took a sip of her coffee, quizzical eyes centered on her daughter. "By the way, you haven't mentioned the rehearsal last night. How did it go?"

Instant gloom. "Not so well."

To her surprise, her mom burst into laughter. "If you could only see your face. It practically droops. That bad, huh?"

"That bad. No one seems interested, or even cares."

"Guess I shouldn't be laughing. Don't forget, young people have a lot on their minds these days. Trying to fit in, dealing with social media, anxiety and that's just to name a few concerns. It'll be up to you to make them understand the importance of the Christmas story. Maybe it will inspire them so they can go on and inspire others."

"Good idea, Mom. And you're right as usual. How to make them understand is another matter."

"Don't underestimate your students. They are all good at heart."

Serena wasn't so sure. Images of a doll's head rolling across the room made her feel less than enthusiastic about her mom's attempts to console and support her.

"I'll keep trying."

Mary reached over and grabbed her hand. "I know you will. You're doing this for me, and I'm so sorry to put you through it all. If you want, please go back to school. I'll get by."

"It's okay, Mom. You've been here for me in a million ways. Now it's my turn."

"Don't get me wrong, I appreciate your help, but maybe it's time I retire. Maybe it's time to give in. To shut the place down."

Serena watched a cloud of worry flit through her mother's eyes and squeezed her hand.

"You are way too young to retire and besides, you know you don't want to. And it's not just a bakery, Mom. It's where meetings are held, showers, weddings. It's a happy place and one of the mainstays of the town. And it's also a place to mourn and heal. Angel's heart, so to speak. We must keep on fighting for it. It's now a piece of town history."

She had prayed nonstop for help ever since she moved back. She hadn't lost hope yet, believing she still had a stab at it if she got a full-time job.

"It's kind of you to say that, but it still bothers me that you gave up your studies. You worked hard to get this far and you're so close to graduation."

"I didn't give them up, Mom. I can still research and work from here online. The bakery means a lot to me, as well. And I was going to end up teaching soon anyway." She glanced at her watch. "But I have to run. I'll do some baking when I get back."

"Are you still helping Pastor Smythe by taking Sunny to her riding lesson?"

"Yes. Is it okay? Do you need me here?"

"No, I'm fine. And don't think I didn't notice that you made an extra batch of reindeer cookies last night because you were going to be gone this morning. Love their quirky smiles and happy faces."

"Just wanted to help. Besides, driving Sunny is just a one time shot." She glanced at her watch again. "And I'd better get a move on."

"Well, have fun."

"I will." Serena picked up her dishes and took them to the kitchen. Glancing out the window over the sink, she noticed it was still dark and star-glittered patterns wove in and out across the sky. She stared up at the heavens.

"Please guide me, God. This is all about You, so please help me pull off this pageant. Please, please, please."

Could she get her students to appreciate the real meaning of Christmas and how important the pageant was?

She had to try. She had to make them understand.

However, first things first.

She had an errand to do.

Six

"Come on, Holly," crooned Serena, opening the gate leading to the room where the dogs were playing. An area behind the kitchen had been turned into a pet haven, so Gloria felt comfortable when her mom worked at the bakery. Soft comfy dog beds lined one wall, a basket of toys sat dead center, and water and food bowls were scattered about. Holly claimed it as her own, as well. She was lucky. It looked so inviting, Serena wanted to curl up on one of their beds herself.

Her dog ran out, barking with excitement, tail wagging fast. She loved adventures.

"We're on a mission, girl. See you later, Gloria. Sorry you can't come."

The golden retriever gave a longing look at her furry friend, but recognised her place was with her mother. Serena knew Gloria hated being away from her, or else she'd have brought her along.

Leashing Holly, she led her out the back door and around to her car on the main street. She couldn't very well scoot through the bakery for obvious hygienic reasons. Opening the door, her tiny dog jumped in the back seat where Serena placed her in her little car seat, keeping her secured and safe.

"Yeah, yeah, I know you hate being restrained," she said. "But it's for your own good and hey, we're going to go visit a farm."

Holly raised her head high and let out a long howl of joy.

Serena laughed as she settled herself in the driver's seat.

"You're going to love it there. I phoned the ranch and the girl who answered said it was okay to bring you. But you have to stay near me and be good."

Holly's series of quieter yips and yaps sounded as if she were talking, promising to be on her best behavior.

"Yeah, right. I know you. You'll have your nose in everything because I bet there are a million sniffs there for you to explore. But you must behave. I even brought a special bone for you to chew, to keep you busy and out of trouble."

Glancing through the back mirror, she smiled. The word bone made Holly wag her tail even faster, hitting the car seat like a drumbeat signaling pure pleasure.

Serena started the car. "Here we go."

Some folks would think she was crazy chatting with her dog as if she were human but, in her eyes, she practically was. She adored Holly, her constant companion during all her years of studying, and her recent break-up with Jon. Jon. A twist of pain squeezed her heart. They had met in a psychology class and had only dated a few months, but to think he had a wife the whole time still hurt. She found out by accident when a fellow student saw them together and told her, just as she started to care for him. The deception hurt, a lot.

Forget it. It was over. Enough.

Focus on your current task instead.

Her pastor had announced on Sunday that he needed someone to drive Sunny Pearson to a horse farm the following Saturday morning. Sunny was a regular customer at the bakery and Serena knew how anxious the girl was to get back on a horse, so she volunteered. Besides, she loved farms. It would do her good and probably clear her head to be out in the fresh air and sunshine for a while.

Slowing down to read a street sign, she saw the word Elm. This was it. This was where Sunny lived.

Turning down the road, she spotted the young girl on the porch, huge grin, long dark hair, pink cowboy hat perched on her head, cane in hand.

Serena waved as she pulled to a stop and jumped out of the car.

"Hi, Sunny."

"Howdy, Serena."

"Are you ready to go?"

"Sure am."

"Need some help?"

"Nope. I'm good with the cane." Sunny smiled. "Lots of practice."

Serena held the door as the young girl easily navigated the stairs and slid in. "I'm in and out of my parents' car so often, it's easy now." She then turned to greet a happy, squawking Holly who loved nothing more than to meet new people.

Serena slowly closed the door and hurried back to the driver's seat. She turned to look at Sunny.

"I love how excited you are. Love your cowboy hat, too."

"Always wanted a pink one," Sunny said. "And Mom gave me this yesterday in celebration of my return to riding."

"What a thoughtful gift. It's gorgeous." Serena started the car and headed out. "And your leg's doing better?"

"Oh, much better. But I haven't been on a horse since my accident. I'm nervous but excited. Thanks for taking me, though. By next week I'll be able to drive again. My doctor wants one final check in a few days and he'll okay it, thank goodness. My parents run a cleaning business and are busy most days, so it's hard getting around."

Apparently, or so the pastor had told her because Sunny didn't talk about it much, she was an avid rider until one day the horse she was riding had tripped, and she'd fallen off. The horse was okay, but Sunny had broken her leg in three places. She spent almost a year undergoing intense physiotherapy and was now ready to roll, having fully healed. She was one of the most positive, upbeat people Serena had ever met, always having a smile on her face.

Keep her safe, Lord, please keep her safe.

"No problem," Serena said. "You don't need to thank me. I'm happy you get to do what you love and please let me know whenever you need a ride."

"Awwww...thanks. I'm looking forward to getting back to school and not doing classes online anymore." Sunny touched her arm. "But hey, how's your mother? I know she's using a cane too for almost the same reason. Extra help just to be sure."

Serena grinned. "She's doing great as well."

"Good to know. We both have the same physiotherapist. I've met her there a few times."

"Well, she's doing a fine job with the two of you." Serena glanced over, noting the huge smile on Sunny's face. "By the way, does the horse farm know your history? Is it the one you always go to?"

"Yes." Sunny clapped her hands in excitement. "A lot of the same staff are there, but there's a new owner who knows the scoop and is going to personally supervise me today. I met him and he's a cool dude. He's introduced several new classes and even has specialty ones for the disabled."

Serena knew that someone had taken over the reins of Pleasant Day Farms. It had been quite the news' story for a few weeks and the topic of conversation by everyone who visited the bakery. Apparently, the original owners retired due to health issues, sold the whole farm and moved to Arizona seeking a drier climate much better for them. She'd heard that numerous programs were added by the new owner and several instructors had been hired. Maybe she should consider taking a class herself if she could find the time. She used to ride as a kid but hadn't done it in years. Maybe it'd be good for her.

"How nice," added Serena. "He definitely sounds quite brilliant and innovative."

"Yeah, he's nice, too. I'm even riding Sugar, the horse I was on when I fell."

"Will that be okay?"

"Well, I've been visiting all year whenever I can, keeping my close bond with her. It wasn't her fault someone let a firecracker off and scared her. I was just grateful she didn't get hurt."

"You're right. It wasn't Sugar's fault. Sounds like the work of a trouble-maker." She hadn't realized that was what had happened. "Did they ever catch who did it?"

"Yes, they did. Can't remember his name, but it was some ten-year-old who didn't want to take lessons. They're from another town, too, not here in Angel."

"Hope he learned his lesson."

"He did. He got grounded for ages and had to do lots of community volunteer work. Oh look..." Sunny pointed straight ahead. "Snow is starting to fall."

"Looks pretty, too. James Simon, the weather reporter, isn't predicting much, though. I checked out his newscast this morning." Serena watched the flakes hit the road, then disappear. "Are you comfortable riding in the snow? That is, if we get more? Is it safe?"

"Oh, no, I won't be outside at all. Inside only, in the arena. Doctor's orders."

"Oh, of course. I forgot they have an indoor space."

"And a large one, at that."

"Good to know."

Serena headed out of town, turned onto a country road, then drove a few minutes until she saw the sign, Pleasant Day Farm, depicting a huge shining sun hovering over a magnificent chestnut colored horse. She turned right and navigated down the lane to the farm. She had never been there and was surprised at how beautiful and soothing it appeared. Very picturesque, with a homey, rambling red brick house as its focus, three large barns, one horse arena and plenty of surrounding land to ride on. Framed by slow-falling snowflakes the size of dimes, everything around her also glistened, much like the stars she'd seen earlier today. She wished she'd brought her camera to capture what looked like a Christmas postcard. It was also a perfect day. Cold but bearable.

Serena tore her eyes away from such beauty and parked on a lot near the arena. She hopped out of the car and held the door open for Sunny.

"Need a hand getting out?"

"Nope, I'm good."

Serena opened the back door for Holly, who yapped her approval. She quickly lifted her out of her seat, grabbed her leash, clipped it on and, keeping a tight hold on it, let her out of the car. Her dog was fearless, loved to explore and would bound off in any direction she randomly chose if Serena didn't watch her.

"Are you okay in the snow?" she asked Sunny, not wanting to hover, but also wanting the girl to know she was there for her. Besides, the path leading to the arena was covered with a thin layer of the wet stuff.

"Sure am. I've lots of experience. Don't worry, I won't slip."

On further inspection, Serena realized, as she followed Sunny down the path, that what she had thought were clumps of snow was salt. She directed Holly to trot along on the path beside the walkway to avoid the white pellets.

Suddenly the arena door flew open and out walked, of all people, Matt Jenkins.

Serena's heart flip flopped so fast she hoped there was a defibrillator around. She might need it. Truth be told, she hadn't been able to think about anything else but him since she had last seen him at the school. She had a hard time admitting even to herself how often he was on her mind.

Holly started to whine and pull at her leash. Serena looked down. Her dog's eyes were centered on Matt.

Oh, no.

She knew that look.

Holly had this habit of taking instant likings to certain people, like a schoolgirl having a huge crush on someone. It was embarrassing, and apparently, she liked Matt a whole lot right now. Immediately. On the spot.

Serena knew the signs.

First her little dog whimpered, then let out a huge howl, and before Serena could get a stronger grip, Holly yanked the leash out of her hand and ran over to Matt. Barking with obvious delight, she stood in front of him, dancing on her hind legs as if to catch his attention, then rolled around in the snow, stirring up gravel and dirt buried underneath. She emerged filthy, muddy, and much to Serena's embarrassment, jumped up, placing her dirty paws on Matt's jeans, barking again, begging for his attention.

It was quite a comical spectacle on one hand, but also awkward as anything.

Sunny burst into laughter. Jade came running over, obviously hearing the barking and wondering what was going on. Matt just looked stunned.

"That was quite a show. What does your dog want?" he asked, reaching down to pat Holly on the head.

"Um, to be picked up. But please don't. She's filthy." She pulled out the doggy treat she had in her pocket. "Here's your bone. Come and get it."

Holly completely ignored her.

"No problem," Matt said.

Immediately he scooped the tiny dog up, cuddling her in his arms.

Oh no. Serena was mortified at the filthy paw marks now streaking his coat as well.

"So sorry. She's leaving clumps of dirt smudges all over you."

"Don't worry. They'll wash off." And he continued to pet Holly.

Serena had to admit, it touched her heart to see her little dog licking his face in pure genuine happiness. Her mom's words rang in her ears, *"A real pet lover is a person to cherish."* Not to mention, he looked good in jeans, blue plaid jacket and cowboy hat.

Now why did she have to go and notice that?

Cherish him?

No way.

Not only did she not like him, but she had no time to care for someone even if she wanted to. Which she didn't. Not after that Jon debacle. She had only one quest at the moment which was to save her mother's bakery. That was the most important thing in her life.

And of course, save the Christmas pageant, which was key in all of that.

She ignored the fact that Matt infiltrated her dreams on a nightly basis.

Stop thinking about him.

"What are you doing here?" she asked, trying to ignore how handsome he looked. "Is Jade riding, too?"

He smiled. "I live here."

"You do?"

"Yes."

"He's my instructor," Sunny said.

Startled, Serena jumped. She had forgotten about Sunny completely. Great, since she was the sole reason she was here.

Matt scratched Holly on her head. "Today, anyway. I just want to make sure everything goes well for your first ride. Welcome back." He smiled at Sunny and her eyes lit up.

But wait a second.

Sunny said the owner was her instructor today.

Matt was the owner?

Although she'd listened to people talking about the farm, she'd never heard his name mentioned in connection with it. Or it just hadn't registered.

"Oh well, great," Serena said, realizing they were both staring at her. She hoped Matt hadn't clued into how captivated she was by his eyes, as blue as the sky behind him.

"Well, we should get started. Here's your dog." Matt pulled Holly away from clutching onto him and handed her over. The dog twisted and turned to keep her eyes trained on Matt, still star struck. "Cute pup."

Next, he said to Sunny, "Let's get going." He led her into the barn.

Serena glanced over at Jade, who stood there, taking it all in. "How are you doing?"

She squatted down to pet Holly. "Okay, I guess. Were you the one who called to ask if you could bring your dog?"

"Yes. Was that you who answered?"

"It was me. I thought I recognized your voice. What's your dog's name?"

"Holly."

She looked up. "So, you love Christmas? Is that why she's called Holly?"

"Yes, I do love Christmas and that's exactly why I called her Holly. How about you? Is it your favorite season, too?"

Serena registered the sadness that filled her eyes.

"It's all right."

Come to think of it, Serena scanned the area...there were no Christmas decorations or any signs of the festive season. Maybe they hadn't put them up yet? Or were they just not interested in doing so?

"So how do you think the play is coming along?" She changed the subject fast, not wanting to upset Jade any further.

Jade stood up, giggling. "Don't want to insult you or anything, but it's a mess."

Serena grinned. "You're right. I'm hoping it'll get better in time."

"Maybe, if we can get through at least one rehearsal without the doll falling." She shook her head. "Jacob's a fun guy, though. And actually, really nice. He just seems to act silly at times."

"It's good to hear about the kinder side of him."

Did the girl blush? Hmmm...was there a crush going on here?

"Oh, and Julie called me last night," added Jade, enthusiastically. "We chatted for a while and she seems pretty cool."

"Well, that's just great. She's a lovely girl."

"Sure is. Hey, wanna go for a walk?" Jade asked. "I could show you around."

Serena noticed how excited she was. She seemed to be enjoying having some company. "That's a wonderful idea. I planned on taking Holly for a walk while I wait for Sunny."

"Well, we've got lots of space here for your dog to run."

Jade led her around the arena and out back. The snow was deep, but it looked like a small truck or tractor with a snow blade had snaked through a wooded area, clearing a path. Serena unleashed Holly, who was loving her freedom, running and jumping and burrowing through the snow. They walked in silence, laughing at Holly's escapades, and eventually they came to a bend that led back along the house.

Serena noticed a sign. She moved closer to take a look. *Matthew Jenkins, attorney-at-law.*

"Is your dad practicing here?"

"Yes. He works from home. He turned two rooms in the back into an office."

"And he runs the farm, too?"

"Well, he has the man who helped before, James Reid, overseeing the horses, lessons and rides. He also has lots of instructors. Dad kept them all on when he took over this place and even hired a few more. Mostly he's a lawyer, but he works in the barn when he can. He's had loads of experience since he's been riding his whole life." She grinned. "He loves horses, sometimes even more than me, and enjoys teaching here and there. But usually, he's in his office with clients and paperwork."

A brilliant set-up. Kind of a modern-day cowboy. He did what he wanted, the best of both worlds, and provided a good wholesome upbringing for his daughter.

"Oh, I'm sure he loves you more than horses," Serena quickly said, realizing she hadn't responded.

Jade laughed. "Yeah, guess he does. I'm just kidding. Er, did you find a singer for the pageant yet?"

"Not yet." Serena loved how when Jade laughed, her whole face lit up. Unfortunately, at school, she rarely even smiled.

"Sorry. I feel like I'm letting you down."

"Oh, no, you're not at all."

Serena was still curious. What exactly were all the problems with the singing? She'd love to get to the bottom of that. "You said your mother sang?"

"Yes, all the time. She died well over a year ago. Actually, it'll be two years soon."

The young girl's eyes darkened with emotion. Serena could feel her intense pain.

"I'm sorry to hear that. You must miss her a lot."

"Yeah, I do. Lots."

"Did you sing with her?"

"Sure did. At home, when we jammed together, and also at church. We were in the choir together. But Dad hates God now, so we don't go."

"He does?"

"Yeah. For taking my mom away."

"Do you feel that way, too? Is that why you don't want to sing?"

"Nah. I'm okay with God." She paused. "It's Dad who doesn't want me to sing, not me."

"Did he actually say that?"

"Kinda, and I see the pain in his eyes whenever I do sing, so I keep my mouth shut around him."

"Oh." Serena wanted to ask more about her mother and why her dad didn't want her to sing but stayed quiet, feeling she had to tread lightly in this area. She sensed hesitation from Jade and probably needed to gain more of her trust before she would truly open up. "What's your favorite Christmas song?"

Maybe changing the subject might help. To reassure Jade she wasn't prying.

"Silent Night."

"Love that song, too. Would you mind?"

"Mind what?"

"Would you mind singing it?"

She grinned. "Right now?"

"Yes. Only if you want to, of course. I love your voice."

"Well, okay."

Jade raised her head and as the first few notes of the carol spilled out, it was obvious how much she loved to sing. Her eyes continued to glow, and a sense of peace enveloped her. She was in another world as her soft voice grew in intensity.

Serena's heart melted.

Her tone was just as she remembered it, perfectly on key and hauntingly angelic.

It was powerful.

Tears trickled down.

The young girl's gift was filled with such beauty it touched her, and once again, she felt it was an honor to listen. She was one special person, this Jade. Serena hoped she would get to know her better and figure out the problem with the singing. Maybe even convince her to give it a try in public again or convince Matt to let her.

No way should her gift be hidden from the world.

Seven

"Good job, Sunny." Matt watched her climb down off her horse, ready to step in if needed. She looked well in control as she pulled her adjustable cane out of her back pocket and extended it so she could use it to walk.

"Do you think so?"

"Yes, I do." He noted her flushed face and excited eyes. She loved to ride, that was a given. "You'll be competing again before you know it."

"Thank you. I hope so. I'm going to brush down Sugar's coat now, is that okay? Am I finished with my lesson?"

"Yes, you are. Go right ahead."

"Okay. And thanks for helping me today."

"No problem. You are quite the skilled rider."

She beamed, and it was all he could do to stop himself asking if she was able to take care of the horse, realizing she could or wouldn't have suggested it. She seemed determined to not let her injury keep her down. Good for her. Her courage and strength were impressive. He could certainly learn from her example.

Silent night. Holy night...

Matt stopped in his tracks.

Even through the walls of the arena, Sunny's laughter, horses snorting and people chatting nearby, he would know that voice anywhere.

It was Maya's.

Beautiful, strong and pure.

Don't be ridiculous.

It couldn't be her.

It was Jade and her voice sounded more like Maya's every time he heard it.

Maya.

A stab of pain hit him.

All is calm. All is bright...

Guilt still surged whenever he thought of his wife and how he had let her down. He had been so busy trying to make it in the business world, pushing hard to provide for his family and give them everything they ever wanted, or at least what he thought they wanted. In fact, he had neglected one major aspect key to family life. He hadn't spent much time being a good husband and father. Instead, long hours in the office claimed him. Maya was fine with that at the beginning of their marriage, but when Jade arrived and her own singing career took off, she felt overwhelmed trying to hold it all together. She had also expressed feelings of loneliness, coping with his constant absenteeism from home. He kept promising to leave work earlier to spend more time with them, also to attend her upcoming shows.

He lied.

Singing. Concerts.

The career journey that killed her.

Round yon virgin, mother and child...

So yes, he loved his daughter's voice, but he didn't want her following the same path as his wife. It was too risky. He couldn't afford to lose her, too. That was why, when this farm had come up for sale, he had given up his practice and moved here to start fresh. To give his daughter a more wholesome upbringing in a small community. He'd loved it here when he was young, but had moved away during the spring of his eighth grade, after his dad was transferred to a bank in Chicago. It was a great place for Jade to be. Safer, anyway. At least he hoped so. He also enjoyed reconnecting with horses, a world he used to love and had left behind.

Holy Infant, so tender and mild...

And here she sang. With the voice of an angel. Just like her mother. Even amid sadness, he couldn't help but be proud.

"Hey, James," he shouted over to the man cleaning the arena. "Be back in a minute."

"No problem. Is that your daughter singing?"

"Yes."

"What a beautiful voice."

"Thank you. I'll let her know what you said."

He'd heard compliments too many times to count, he figured, as he took off out of the arena, searching for Jade.

Sleep in Heavenly Peace...

Speaking of heaven and angels, he hoped Serena didn't hear her. She'd be recruiting her again for the Christmas show. He'd been a shepherd in that exact play back when he was a kid, and he knew the song "O Holy Night" was a huge part of it. A tradition that obviously continued, unless it was "Silent Night" now.

Serena.

Had to admit he still felt something for her.

She'd broken his heart way back in elementary school, when she'd gotten angry and stopped speaking to him. All because she'd thought he'd done something to humiliate her. He hadn't. She had misunderstood and wouldn't listen when he'd tried to explain. Sure, he was just a kid back then, and didn't know what love was, but it had cut to the quick. They say your first love is never forgotten, no matter how young you are. Whoever *they* were had gotten it right. It had been a school kid's devotion, but still powerful.

And there she was. He'd finally found her.

His daughter.

Standing with Serena, framed by swirling snowflakes, eyes closed, arms outstretched, belting out the Christmas carol, pouring her whole heart into the music. The visual was breathtaking and her stunning voice, heavenly.

He stood still watching her. Mesmerized. Even the little dog stared at his daughter, as if hanging on to every note. Jade was in her element, so caught up in the song. It moved him, was an honor to watch, a showstopper.

As she continued with the verses, he shifted his eyes to Serena.

She was still so beautiful, both inside and out.

Sunny had explained how Serena had driven her there out of the goodness of her heart. Once again, his thoughts were filled with all the ways she'd helped others, taking care of them, making their lives easier. Each day he remembered more examples, for after they'd stopped speaking, he used to watch her from afar. She was the first to sit by the new kids in the school and make them feel welcomed, the first to volunteer to assist someone, the first to comfort someone sad. It was who she was, and he admired her for that.

Stop it. Enough about her.

It wasn't as if they were going to reconnect or anything, even if she were open to it, which he was sure she wasn't. She had never been interested in him.

Besides, dating was a thing of the past for him.

Six months earlier, he had made a brief attempt, thinking it might alleviate his pain, but quickly lost interest. The first woman seemed to view his daughter as competition for his attention, and the second one made it clear she never wanted children, in fact didn't seem to even like them. So, he gave up. After all, it hadn't been that long since Maya had passed away and he had Jade to raise. That was all that was important.

He would never find love again. He didn't deserve it and God wouldn't allow it. He was convinced of this.

God.

He used to believe. Not so much anymore.

No way should his wife have died so unnecessarily.

She deserved more. Way more.

Jesus, Lord at thy birth...

As the last notes of the song drifted away, he was still amazed at the loveliness of his daughter's voice and the emotion she poured into it.

Maya used to say it was better than hers. His wife's was electrifying, but Jade's was just so pure, so stunning, it left you wanting more.

He'd have to watch his daughter closely and keep her safe and out of the path of harm. It was the most important mission in his life.

What?

Something tugged at the hem of his jeans.

Looking down, he saw Serena's dog, staring up at him, adoration in her eyes. Guess he'd been so engrossed in his thoughts; he hadn't seen her run over.

"Hello there, little one," he said, smiling at her huge dose of adorableness.

The dog barked, twirled round and round and then jumped, placing her paws once again on his knees.

"Do you want me to pick you up?"

Her little tail wagged as he reached down for her. She snuggled into his arms for the second time that day.

"Holly, where are you?" yelled Serena, sounding worried.

"She's right here." Matt carried her over.

"Oh, so sorry. She's bugging you again."

"No problem." He turned to his daughter. "Honey, loved your version of 'Silent Night.' You sound amazing."

"Thanks, Dad."

After handing Holly back to Serena, he ignored the look of hope in her eyes. He knew she wanted him to okay Jade singing in the pageant.

Sorry. He couldn't do that.

No way.

His sole objective was to take care of his daughter, and keeping her secure was his goal.

And no one, not even Serena, was going to interfere.

Eight

Oh, no. Not again, thought Matt.

After Serena's visit to the farm the other day, he struggled harder to push thoughts of her out of his mind. Considering she was all he could think about, besides his daughter, he wasn't doing a good job.

Was that really her?

Serena the ballerina?

Funny how that old nickname stuck, even though he knew now she had hated it. He'd once thought it was sweet, even complimentary, because it was true. In elementary school, everyone knew she danced and besides, the two words rhymed—Serena and ballerina. Sort of.

He squinted.

Yes, it was her.

She was like a shadow he couldn't seem to shake. Guess living in a small town made it more likely to see the same people frequently, but it frustrated him. Thinking about her disturbed his life and not in a good way, either. He didn't want to keep re-living his past and having it infiltrate his present. He had too many other things to focus on.

He also couldn't keep his eyes off her.

Matt was parked outside the church, waiting for his daughter to exit. His sister, Irena, had made a surprise visit to the ranch and had taken Jade to church with her. Since it had snowed overnight and Irena had yet to put on snow tires, he'd dropped them off and was here to pick them up. Serena was one of the first to leave, bursting through the front door and hurrying down the street, her long hair flying behind. He remembered how she used to be teased about its color, sporting the nicknames Flame and Red as well as ballerina. It was darker now, a deep rich auburn, just as stunning as always. She also walked as if on tippy toes wearing ballet shoes. Was she? He looked. Nope, boots. Silly to think she was. She literally glowed and moved with such grace, he found himself completely enthralled. Again.

His heart pounded.

Exactly what he didn't want to feel.

He wished he could avoid seeing her.

No matter what, they seemed to run into each other. He'd spotted her in the local grocery store just last night and later on, walking down the main street.

He even found himself looking for her. Reconnecting had brought up a longing to talk to her, a yearning he didn't welcome as he found himself taking steps towards her, then backing away fast. Almost tripping over his feet. Ever since she'd been to his home, he'd even gotten into the habit of staying up late reading, hoping he'd forget about her.

Not possible.

He felt lost in a mass of hope and sadness.

And memories.

Just as if it were yesterday, he recalled how, as a seventh grader, he had finally gotten up the courage to wait for her after school one day. He planned to walk her home and tell her how much he liked her. Maybe even get to hold her hand. He remembered it clearly for it was right before the Halloween dance and he'd been hoping she'd go with him. Not as a date, but as good friends. Instead, she'd walked out of the school with Billy Leith, laughing at something he said, and he'd slunk away, never to try again. He had no chance against Billy, who was smart, a star soccer player and girls seemed to hang on his every word. He hadn't even gone to the dance at all, staying home, watching a movie, wondering if she were there with Billy.

Then there was that mess of a Christmas pageant. And how she blamed him for what happened.

"Hey, open the door," yelled his sister, banging on the window.

So engrossed with watching Serena, he hadn't even noticed his sister had arrived. He quickly jumped out and opened the door for Jade and Irena.

Unlike Matt, his sister had maintained friendships in Angel when they'd left town and had continued visiting, since she lived nearby. This was good for Jade, for she loved Irena and liked the idea of seeing her more. Not so great for him. He loved his sister, but she was so blunt at times, it was tough dealing with her. Like her goal to get him dating again.

"It's been long enough. You're young. Get out there and try again," she kept saying. She constantly tried to hook him up with friends until one night, urged on by frustration, he set her straight.

"I'm not looking for anyone," he had yelled, then stormed away. After that, she kept quiet.

"It's a shame you didn't come into the church and sit with us," Irena said, getting in the car.

There was her outspokenness again.

"Maybe another time," he said, trying to appease her as well as stop her from bugging him. She'd started on him the minute she'd woken up that morning and found out he wasn't going, so he had taken off to the stable to help with lessons, just to get away from her.

"I told you, he's not into God since Mama died," announced Jade.

"Is that true?" asked Irena. "Is that when you stopped going?"

"Maybe."

"Well, you can't blame God forever. It's not His fault. It was a horrid situation, but you should thank God Maya is in no pain now, and that her kidnapper is in jail."

He looked out the window, not even bothering to answer. It still hurt too much.

It wasn't true that he completely blamed God. Well, guess he did since Maya's death was so senseless, but in fact, he blamed himself more. He had let his wife down and didn't feel worthy of God's love. After all, it was his fault his wife had died, and as he told himself daily, he *should* feel guilty about what had happened. He knew he'd treated her poorly and deserved to feel awful for the rest of his life. It was his penance. He was heartbroken she had died, but had been told right after she'd arrived at the hospital that she probably wouldn't make it. At least she was in no more pain. Thank goodness her kidnapper had been arrested and was in jail for life, or he would have stalked him until he found him, even if he had landed in prison himself. The only thing going for him now was Jade. She was his life.

He was also glad Irena finally stayed quiet, hopefully sensing by his silence it was not a topic he wanted to discuss.

"Hey Dad, can we get some donuts? Remember how we used to always get them with Mom after church and pig out. Please?"

"Oh, I remember all right. Your mother had the biggest sweet tooth going and I know you take after her. Good idea. Let's do it. Is there still a bakery around here, sis? I vaguely remember one in town."

"There's one just down the road. Keep going, now slow down. Right here. Pull over."

He came to a stop and looked at the sign on the red brick building. Petals Café and Bakery. He also noticed the for-sale sign below it.

"Oh, I remember coming in here for the best chocolate chip cookies ever. They always used both dark and white chocolate."

"Haven't been in here for a while, but I bet they still have them," Irena said.

"Good." He jumped out, held the door for them and they walked into the bakery. Immediately he was hit with the mouth-watering aromas of chocolate and freshly baked bread drifting around him, as if competing for his attention. The answer was simple. It was a tie. He glanced at the counter, searching for the cookies, finding them stacked and ready.

"Hey, Daddy, they even have my favorite, cinnamon buns," his daughter said, running over to the glassed-in showcase. "Oh, look at all that icing. I like them even more than donuts."

Matt smiled at the excited look in his daughter's eyes.

"They do look good. So, we'll get you one."

"Yay! Can we stay here and eat?" Jade asked. "It's a pretty cool café." She was busy checking out all the nutcrackers lined around the room in various hues of colors and sizes.

"Of course, we can." He nodded. "Looks like a nice place to hang out in."

"There are seats over there." Irena pointed across the room. "Lucky us. Right by the window." She led their small parade further into the store.

No sooner were they seated than a pleasant looking older woman greeted them with a smile. "Welcome to Petals. My name is Helen. May I help you?"

"Yes, thank you. What would you like, honey?" Matt asked, chuckling at his daughter's huge eyes which were again glued to the counter, checking out the various baked goods. "Still the cinnamon bun?"

"Yes, I'd like one of those and also a chocolate donut with sprinkles and a chocolate milk. Can I have a cookie too, Dad? To take home?"

"Well, okay, but pace yourself. If you eat all that at once, you'll get sick."

"Okay. I'll just have the cinnamon bun first."

"I can box the rest, if you'd like." Helen's smile grew larger.

"That would be wonderful." Matt smiled back. "Please add two chocolate chip cookies."

"Make it three," Irena said. "They look good."

"I'll have a coffee, as well," Matt added. "You, too, Irena?"

"Yes, definitely, and a cinnamon bun to eat right here. Matt, you must try one. They're to die for."

"Okay. You don't have to ask me twice."

As an amused Helen walked away, having listed their order on a notepad, he looked around.

No way.

His breath caught in his throat.

Was that really Serena coming in a side door, twisting her hair up into a net and tying on an apron?

Are you kidding me?

Again?

"Does she work here?" he asked.

"Who?" His sister turned to look. "Oh, Serena. Of course, she does. Her mother owns this place. Didn't you know that?"

She did?

"Guess I didn't, or just never thought about it."

Irena's smile widened. "Wait a second. I seem to recall you having a huge crush on her."

"You had a crush on Ms. Davis?" Jade asked, looking way too interested.

"No, I didn't."

"Yes, he did," Irena said. "I remember how you used to like hanging around her."

"So, Serena teaches and works here as well?" It was a desperate attempt to change the subject before Irena kept going. She loved nothing more than to tease him. He knew it was because she cared but still...

"Yes. According to my sources, Serena's mother broke her leg, and Serena came home to help. She's also teaching to raise money to buy this building. Did you see the for-sale sign outside?"

It made total sense that Serena had dropped everything and come back to help her mother. That was exactly who she was. If times were tough, she would always be right there working to make everything better.

"Yes, I did see the sign, but didn't pay much attention to it." He smiled at Helen who had arrived with their drink order. After she left, he continued, "Actually thought nothing of it, figuring the bakery was either closing voluntarily because Serena's mother was selling it or would stay put when the building was purchased by new owners."

"Nope, the couple wanting to buy the building plan to close it."

Matt watched Irena pour milk into her coffee mug, along with two teaspoons of sugar. He'd forgotten about her love of milky, sugary hot drinks.

"Apparently Serena's mother doesn't want to shut down," she added. "She's being forced to."

"I'm surprised the locals would let this place go," Matt said. "From what I recall, now that I'm thinking back to my elementary days, it's the only bakery in town, right?"

"Yes, it's one of a kind and a shame it might all end." Irena pointed to the showcase. "It's such a great place, with every treat imaginable and a gathering spot for everyone."

Jade leaned over and whispered, "That must be her mom over there with the boot on. She's using a cane."

"Yes, sweetie, that's her." Irena waved at her. "But she's okay now. She just needs some help until she's completely healed. You'll probably be interested to know Serena also teaches ballet. Didn't you use to do that?"

"Used to," Jade answered. "I took lessons for years. Hmmm, so she teaches a dance class."

"You could always ask if she's taking on new students," suggested Irena.

Oh, no, thought Matt. Jade quit ballet when her mother passed away. She just seemed to lose all interest. He hoped she didn't get any more thoughts about dancing again. These Serena meetings were unsettling, and he didn't want more encounters with her, if he could help it. Especially ones where he might have to talk to her. Besides, dancing put his daughter out there again, possibly for the public to view, and he wanted to avoid that.

Was he being selfish?

Ignoring his daughter's needs?

Don't think about that.

He needed to protect her, right?

Yes, he had to do that.

Hearing Serena's laugh, he turned to watch her.

Once again, he was amazed that she could do so much.

There she was, running around helping customers, pouring coffee, placing baked goods in boxes. He began to wonder if she ever slept, what with the café, school, play and volunteer work. Not to mention dance lessons as well.

He watched her smile, noticing her dimples. He'd forgotten about them. She also had a way of moving, as if every step were carefully choreographed, and he wondered if she still danced herself.

"Here you go." Helen placed their cinnamon rolls down on the table and hurried to the next customer. Matt smiled at Jade's wide eyes, as if she couldn't believe the size of the buns. He heard Serena laugh again and he turned to look. Distracted, he shoved a piece of sticky bun in his mouth.

He had to stop thinking of her.

"Dad, you're supposed to wait," reprimanded Jade.

"For what?"

"You forgot; we have to pray. You know we always do this before we eat."

"Oh, okay. Right."

She reached out to take his hand and Irena's.

"God, thanks for the food, bless Mom and Dad and Auntie Irena. And help Ms. Davis find a singer. And please save this bakery. Amen."

Matt thought it was sweet that she prayed for the bakery, too, but cringed at the singer comment as doubt flooded him again.

Was he wrong to discourage her from singing? And now here he was, hoping she wouldn't want to dance either. Thoughts that he had let her down haunted him from the moment he woke up until he fell asleep at night.

It was not only his daughter he thought about.

His wife was at the top of the list, too.

Images of Maya filled his heart. Her beauty. Her smile. Her kindness. Also, her loneliness, her complaints that he was never around, her sadness.

And then one day she was gone.

Just like that.

No. He wasn't being selfish. Not a chance.

He had to protect his daughter. He couldn't afford to lose her.

Matt just hoped the singer his daughter had prayed for wasn't a sign that she really wanted to perform "O Holy Night."

He just couldn't allow it.

Nine

Not him again, thought Serena as she glanced over at Matt for about the tenth time. She'd seen him sitting in his car outside the church and ignored him. In truth, she was startled to find him there, couldn't handle it, and took off fast, head down. Now, here he was in the bakery. She'd noticed him immediately, chatting with Jade and another woman. His girlfriend perhaps?

Somehow, she didn't like that idea. Also, didn't even like to admit she'd had such a thought.

Oh, forget it.

Matt was nothing to her.

She may have had a bit of a schoolgirl's crush on him when she was little, but that was all in the past. Well, not a crush, more of a huge like. After all, they were just kids, and now he had a grown-up daughter and a perhaps girlfriend. Besides, she was turned off men at the moment. She had enough to deal with.

It was tough seeing him, though.

It was like he was in her face every moment. She watched them hold hands, initiated by Jade, apparently praying. Good to see that even though he was mad at God, he still humored his daughter. Maybe there was hope for him. As frustrated as she was with seeing him again, it also made her sad he was so angry that he would deny Jade the chance to sing. She'd have to pray for him as well. Looked like he needed it.

Don't we all?

She sighed as she scooted into the kitchen to check on her latest batch of cinnamon rolls. She used to be good at baking, but was rusty after all those years of school. Completely out of practice.

She reached down to pull open the oven door.

Oh, no.

Burned.

Her timing had been way off.

She pulled out the pan of buns and placed them on the counter. She wouldn't be able to sell them, but they were still edible if she scraped off the black parts. At least some of them were in decent shape.

Excited barks caught her attention as she looked out the back window to see what Holly and Gloria were up to, giggling at the games they played together. Right now, it was tug of war with a shared toy. Looked like Gloria was winning. They both looked adorable with clumps of snow sticking to their fur. She loved their joy and how they lived in the present moment, savoring every minute.

I should be more like them.

Instead, she was always immersed in worries and issues and problems. Also, in trying to create the perfect pageant so she could be the main candidate for the available teaching job in the new year.

"Thanks for helping, dear," her mother said, coming in from the café.

Tossing her stressed thoughts away, she said, "I'm not much of a help." She pointed to the pan filled with disaster.

"Oh, we'll just scrape off the burnt parts and have them with our tea."

"Great minds think alike." Serena grinned. "A ton of icing and we won't be able to tell."

Her mother stood there, staring at her, smiling.

"What are you grinning at?" Serena asked.

"Oh, just at you. I'm so happy to have you here, especially at Christmas."

"Hey, Mom. You say that every day. Just don't forget that I'm happy to be here with you, too. I wouldn't want to be anywhere else." She hugged her mother tightly, crossing her fingers for luck that everything would work out.

She certainly didn't want to see her mother's dream fritter away.

It had now become her dream as well.

With the café doing better, even though she was sometimes baking late into the night, and the savings she accumulated by giving up her apartment in Boston, things were improving. Now, if she could only raise the money to buy the building with her teacher's salary and her ballet lessons, they could keep things going. Debts would be paid off and enough put up for the down payment and mortgage.

She was back to the same old problem.

She needed a singer.

One who would rock the principal's world and make her the number one pick for the job. Hopefully.

Jade.

She needed Jade.

She would be perfect. Her voice was special and beautiful, and it would make up for the messy re-enactment that just never seemed to improve. She may be wrong, but she sensed the girl wanted to sing, too.

Stubborn Matt.

He was the one holding her back.

It was all his fault, she decided, as anger bubbled up inside her again.

Why couldn't he encourage his daughter to perform "O Holy Night?" It was an honor. One of the top roles in the pageant behind Mary, Jesus and Joseph. Most parents would be proud their son or daughter would enhance the whole Christmas story and touch people's hearts.

Not Matt.

She stamped her foot in frustration.

That's it. I'm not taking no for an answer.

At least she had to try. Again. She was not giving up that easily.

Tilting her head in determination, Serena decided to make the attempt before she chickened out.

"Excuse me, Mom. I have to talk to someone. Can you keep an eye on this new pan of cinnamon rolls? I certainly don't want to burn another batch."

"No problem, honey."

Serena sneaked a brief glance in the mirror to make sure her hair wasn't standing on end, wiped the flour off her nose, smoothed down her apron and marched out of the kitchen and right over to Matt's table. Quickly, before she lost her nerve.

"Hi, Ms. Davis." Jade did a little wave with her hand.

"Hi, there." She looked sweet with white frosting on her lips and pure delight in her eyes.

"You are so lucky to work here. Do you get to eat whatever you want?"

"Definitely." Serena attempted a smile, realizing she probably looked tense. "I'm a big fan of those cinnamon buns, too. Piled high with icing."

"Is there any other way?" Jade laughed. "I'd be eating them all day if I could."

"Sometimes, I do," Serena said, smiling at their banter.

"Hello, I'm Irena," the beautiful blonde-haired woman said, reaching her hand out for a shake.

"Nice to meet you." She could understand why Matt would be taken with her. She was stunning, with long hair and big blue eyes.

Serena turned to Matt.

"May I speak to you for a minute?"

She almost laughed at how panicky he looked, as his eyebrows practically rose to the ceiling.

"Well, okay, I guess." He sounded reluctant. As if he'd rather be doing anything else but spend time with her.

"Not here, though. Come, follow me. Please."

Once again, he looked terrified. Like a mischievous kid about to be scolded. It was quite comical.

Don't laugh, Serena. You need to be serious. This is very important.

Knowing Holly and Gloria were still out playing in the yard, she led him to the dog room to afford them some privacy. When she turned to face him, all she could think of was, *this was a big mistake.*

She'd always laughed at romance books when they described attraction as electrifying, hearts racing, goosebumps, quick intakes of breath, shakiness. Now she finally understood, as she took in his jeans, red plaid shirt, cowboy boots and how good they looked on him. Why, she even felt bolts of what she could only term as lightning race through her. She'd never felt that way about Jon. Or anyone. Ever. Not even once.

Breathe, she thought. In and out. In and out. Please, don't pass out. Could you imagine? Fainting at his feet?

Guess those mushy books and movies were true. With the right person, it was magical. Breathtaking.

Wait a second.

Right person?

What was she thinking?

He was *not* the right person for her.

Just why did he have to be so attractive, though, with blue eyes watching her, and the hair that never seemed to stay in place flopping down his forehead. It was all she could do to stop herself from reaching up and pushing it back.

Her breath quickened. Again.

Stop it.

How ridiculous to feel anything other than anger.

This was the guy who had broken her heart in elementary school and made her a laughingstock. Not only by not liking her back, but by how he treated her at their own pageant.

He was not someone to be trusted. In the least.

"Do you need something?" he asked. "Is that why you wanted to talk to me?"

Her face reddened.

Had he caught her checking him out? Did he sense it? Feel it?

"What? Oh, yes." She pulled herself out of her dangerous thoughts to remember why they were there. "Please, will you let Jade sing?"

Silence. His eyes flicked out the window, then back at her.

"Sorry, not trying to be difficult, but no. Absolutely not."

"Why?"

"I have my reasons."

"But why have a gift and not use it? And Jade has incredible talent. She should be sharing it for the glory of God, at least."

Darn. She shouldn't have mentioned God, she thought, as his eyes darkened in anger. Wrong choice of word and sentiment. He probably felt she was trying to guilt him into letting Jade sing. Or manipulate him. And in a way, he'd be right. She was.

"God took away my wife. And she was one of the good people. Someone who gave and gave and gave. It still didn't keep her alive. There is no glory here."

"But..."

"No buts. She's not singing. The matter is closed."

He turned and stormed away. Well, he didn't really storm, but the effect was the same.

So that was it. He did blame God. Jade was right.

He needed prayers desperately.

Come to think of it, so did she.

It hit her hard that she was fast losing all perspective on this nativity scene, so preoccupied with doing it right for her mother and this bakery, and not for God.

She had to stop. After all, Christmas was supposed to be a joyous occasion.

Desperate was not a good state to be in.

Her uneasiness probably flowed out to her students, helping make it the disaster it was. She had to get her priorities straight. Forget the students ruining the pageant...she did a good job of it herself.

Enough.

She had to get back in focus.

But how?

She just couldn't lose her mom's bakery. She had to save it.

It had become her obsession.

Her mission.

"God," she whispered. "Please guide me. I need your help."

It was all she could think of to say.

She hoped it was enough.

Ten

So, what is the true meaning of Christmas?
And how do I explain it to the children?

Actually, they weren't really children. They were preteen, full of questions and opinions and possibly hard to convince.

How could she get them to understand? Especially since many adults didn't. Maybe even herself.

It was all Serena could think about.

Except for Matt. She was thinking way too much about him lately, but trying hard to block him out of her mind.

Without much luck.

Especially since it was obvious he was angry with her for persistently wanting Jade to sing. Yes, she pushed. She just couldn't help it.

Yesterday, when she had arrived home from work, she'd discovered that Sunny had left a message to say she had lost a hair barrette in her car. It had been a gift from her grandmother and one she treasured, so after a complete search, Serena found it tucked under Holly's car seat. She made arrangements to take it to her house and leave it in her mailbox.

Driving there before school started took her down country roads, leaving her plenty of time to reflect on the school pageant. It also helped that on the way back, snow drifted down, making her feel fully in the Christmas spirit. All she needed were some holiday carols.

She turned on her radio and "What Child Is This" rang out, enhancing her thoughts about the pageant and wondering how to express them to twelve-year-olds in words they'd understand.

In many ways it seemed silly to reflect on the true significance of Christmas. All her life so far, Serena had celebrated this holiday with her parents, then alone with her mom and grandmother, then just her mom. She enjoyed it, loved the warmth and delight of the season, went to church, celebrated Jesus' birthday, but never stopped to reflect on its whole meaning. It was just a part of her life, a tradition, an event. If you paused to think, it was about the Christ child and sharing and loving and family, but how to get the whole spiritual message across to young people was a whole other matter. She wanted them to feel excited about being part of the nativity scene, proud, and fervently committed to depicting the wonder of that first Christmas morning so long ago. Especially since commercialism was rampant, and the principal wanted them to remember the whole giving side. The caring side. The miraculous side. The real truth behind the birth. It had to be about Jesus, of course, but how can a young person fully grapple with the holy child's importance, especially when adults struggled. And especially since the excitement of getting presents was high on a young person's list. An adult's list, too, unfortunately.

She'd just have to figure out a way.

Finished with her errand and arriving back at work, she pulled into the school parking lot, tossing her Christmas thoughts aside. She had her class to think of and subjects to teach, not to mention photocopies to run off. She'd reflect on the pageant dilemma later. Grabbing her briefcase, she hurried to the side door, careful not to go flying on the wet snow covering the pathway. She'd obviously beaten the caretaker to school, because he was diligent about shoveling. Knowing it was still very early in the day, she rushed into the photocopy room first, hoping to get there before a crowd appeared, and dropped her files on the table.

She was pleased to see Nancy Travis already working away. She'd recognize those long curly black locks, half in a ponytail, half trailing down her back, anywhere.

"Hey, there," Serena said. "Good morning."

"Hey, yourself," Nancy responded, glancing up from the machine. "Good morning to you, too."

"Guess I can never beat you." Serena grinned. "Sometimes I think you sleep here."

"Sometimes I think that, too." She moved a stack of copies from the machine and dropped them on the table, then added more paper.

Nancy had been her very first friend when she'd arrived in Angel at the age of eight. They'd met in dance class and became best friends when the two of them pirouetted the wrong way during rehearsal, collided and ended up falling, legs entangled, giggles erupting. When she went off to college, they'd kept in touch for a while through email, but it slowly dwindled away as time marched on. She was thrilled to reconnect with her and glad to have the support of this wonderful lady when she'd taken the job. In fact, Nancy was the one who had told her about it, for she was also the kindergarten teacher. Her wonderful friend had shown her the ropes around the building, such as where to store her lunch, where to get paper, pens, and other various supplies. Serena may have been a student there, but it was very different being on the other side as a teacher.

"Please tell me," continued Nancy, pulling her hair back off her face and retying it into a ponytail. "How did rehearsal go yesterday? Any improvement?"

Nancy's thick mop of curls never seemed to obey a scrunchie and her signature move was always trying to control it. Serena leaned over to help tighten the band around her friend's hair, just like she used to when they were kids.

"None. As a matter of fact, they're worse, if that is even possible." She backed away and threw her arms up in exasperation. "I was told they all know their lines and their actions, but nope, they don't. And then I discovered this new girl, Jade, can sing and her dad won't let her."

Nancy abruptly stopped photocopying and turned to look at her.

"You're talking about Matt Jenkin's daughter, right? As far as I know, she's the only Jade in the school."

"Right. That's her. I just can't believe he won't let her sing. Her voice is amazing and should be heard, not hidden away." She stopped, noticing Nancy's strange expression. "Hey, why are you looking at me like that?"

"You seriously don't know, do you?"

"Know what?"

"Do you not know who his wife was?"

Why was Nancy's mouth wide open in shock?

"Uh, no. Why would I? I haven't seen nor heard of him in years, so I'd hardly know who he married."

"Well, you've got to be the only one around who hasn't heard of her."

"Well, who is she?"

Nancy paused, clearly emotional, as a tear drifted down her cheek.

"Maya Stone."

Silence.

Then it hit her...

Serena was stunned.

"No way. You mean the singer who wrote the song, 'My star will always be you?' The number one hit for three months a few years ago?"

"Yes. Exactly. She was an up-and-coming country and western singer just about to begin her first state-wide tour."

"Oh, I never knew that. I love her music. I even have one of her CDs. Come on. She was Matt's wife?"

"Yes."

Serena was astonished.

"I thought Jade's voice sounded familiar. It's a lot like her mother's and she did say her mom passed away. I just never connected Maya and Jade together."

"Do you know how Maya passed away?"

"Um, no. I just understand from her school file and from Jade herself, that she had died. I don't know any details."

"Don't you remember how a stalker harassed Maya for months and at her very first concert kidnapped her. When she fought back hard, kicking and screaming, managing to get away in the parking lot, he shot her, yelling that if he couldn't have her no one else could."

Oh, no. Serena dropped onto a chair, sucking in deep breaths. She was in shock and suddenly feeling sick.

"Are you kidding me?"

"No. It was all over the news."

"I vaguely remember some of that, but it must have taken place during a really busy time at school. Besides, I didn't even know she was Matt's wife. I can't believe this just passed me by."

"That's because you moved away and, if I know you, you were probably buried in your books. If you had been here all along, you'd know. For a while, she was in a coma and we had nightly prayer vigils for her, for Matt and for his family, hoping she'd live. It was all anyone talked about for months. I was always a big fan of hers and was devastated when she died."

"Oh, my goodness." Her brain spun, until it finally slowed and she was able to think straight. "No wonder he doesn't want his daughter to sing," she said softly. "He wants to protect her. To stop something like that from ever happening to Jade as well."

"Can't say I blame him. His world was torn apart by music and a stalker. The gossip mill, plus numerous articles written about them, also suggested that Matt blamed himself for not being there for her."

"Unbelievable and so sad. Thanks for telling me. From now on, if I have any questions about a student, I'll ask you."

"And if I can help, I will. Sorry. I would have told you sooner, but I thought you knew. As a matter of fact, I thought I'd emailed you about it, but guess I hadn't."

"Not that I'm aware of. Unless it landed in my spam folder and I never got it. It's so horrible that Matt and Jade lost her and especially like that. So violently."

She suddenly thought of Irena.

"Just curious. Is his new girlfriend a singer too? Has he moved on?"

Nancy looked surprised. "I wasn't aware he had a girlfriend, and news like that would travel fast in Angel. When did you meet her?"

"At Petals. Her name is Irena."

"Blonde hair, blue eyes?"

"Yes, that's her."

Nancy started to laugh. "Girlfriend? That's his sister. Don't you remember? She was a few years younger than us."

Memories surfaced.

"Irena Jenkins. Oh, I vaguely remember that Matt had a sister. Of course. I thought she looked a bit familiar. Same blue eyes, and she used to trail after him all the time."

"Yes, she did."

Now, why did she feel a rush of relief surge through her at the thought he might not have a girlfriend? How totally inappropriate after just finding out who his wife had been.

Nancy glanced at her watch.

"Oops. I'd better get this done or you won't have time to get your own work copied."

"Thanks."

Nancy finished up, said goodbye, and Serena began photocopying.

She just couldn't get Matt off her mind.

She had no idea Maya had been his wife and here she tried to force him to let Jade sing, when he had a good reason to keep her away from doing that very thing.

The bell rang and she bundled up her papers and hurried to class. The whole time she taught, thoughts of Matt crept in. No wonder he was angry at her. She had tried to get his daughter to do something he feared. She'd have to apologize the next time she saw him, considering now she understood his hesitancy.

Like Nancy said, she didn't blame him.

Eleven

"Please everyone. This is a holy moment. All eyes on the baby Jesus," Serena said. "Right now, everyone is looking all over the place, at the ceiling, the walls, each other, and not at the star of the drama. I know it's a doll now, but on the night of the pageant, I want to remind you again we will have a real live baby."

Matt tried not to smile watching Serena attempting to control the class. Not that it was purposely funny, but the re-enactment resembled a comedy show.

He had come early to pick up Jade and had snuck into the back of the church hall to see how the production looked. Mary and Joseph had finally made it through the 'no room at the inn' scene, even though the innkeeper got his lines wrong three times. Then, just as the couple were leaving, the innkeeper's wife had accidentally stepped on Mary's long robe, she tripped, and down she went, banging into Joseph who in turn fell as well, sending the doll representing Baby Jesus flying. During the next twenty minutes, Joseph had dropped the baby Jesus twice more, a shepherd had leaned over to kiss an angel, the Mary character got her robe caught again, this time under a chair and once again tripped, a cow oinked instead of mooed, and the angel holding the star over the cradle was using its shiny material as a mirror to apply lip gloss.

It was so ludicrous he couldn't help the grin inching across his face.

The cast seemed calmer at the moment, listening to what Serena said, but probably not for long. As their teacher said, no one paid attention.

It was far from the sacredness he knew Serena was going for, or the way it should be done. It would be perfect if it were a silly parody, but he felt increasingly bad for Serena, who tried hard to pull it all together. After all, having been in his own pageant, he knew how serious it was supposed to be. He felt like yelling at the cast, but knew it was not his place to do so. He also felt bad for his teacher way back when, who probably put up with a lot from them, too. He remembered giggling during their practices as well.

Stop smiling, he thought.

It was downright rude and if any of them saw him, it could spur them on to be sillier.

Just then, the donkey and cow collided and fell into a heap on the floor. More giggles from the class and more frustration flashed across Serena's face. He'd be tempted to storm out, but she took a few deep calming breaths and continued on, stoic and encouraging. It hit him again how amazing she was.

Finally, they neared the end and he watched Serena lean over and push a button on a CD player.

His heart broke when the sound of "O Holy Night" filled the air. It had been his wife's favorite hymn and he also noted Jade singing along. Sometimes her voice was louder than the one on the CD.

Guilt surged. Again. He should be used to this feeling by now, but he wasn't, and hated when it hit hard, like it did now.

He should have been there the night his wife was kidnapped. He knew she had a stalker who had been slapped with a restraining order by the police, and he had hired a bodyguard to watch her. Apparently during the night of the concert, the guard was distracted by a fire erupting in the change room garbage can and while he struggled to put it out, Maya was grabbed in the hallway. Turned out, the stalker had somehow managed to break into the room earlier and started the fire as a diversion. His intention was to keep the guard busy and deflect from his intent, which was to steal Maya away.

Don't think about that.

But he couldn't stop thinking about it.

He was convinced he could have saved her, believing if he were there that night, he would have never let her out of his sight. Instead, he let his work get in the way as usual. He had meant to attend the concert, but got delayed pushing a deal through to fruition. And his wife had died because of it. He had arrived after she had managed to get away from the kidnapper. She had almost reached the safety of an arena door she could have locked behind her, when she was shot by stalker Jeffrey Arnold. She never regained consciousness and died seven days later.

"Okay, class, that's a wrap," Serena said.

He snapped out of his thoughts.

Shaken, lost in the past, he pushed himself to stand and wave at his daughter, letting her know he was there. She nodded and ran to get her coat, just as Serena spotted him and came over. He was surprised, since he had been rude to her the last time he had seen her. Rude? Who was he kidding? He'd been downright obnoxious. It would be a wonder if she still talked to him at all.

"So how do you think it's going?" She grinned and rolled her eyes.

"The truth?" He smiled back.

"On second thought, please don't tell me. I know, I know. It needs some work. Lots and lots of work. Hey, can I talk to you for a moment?"

"Okay." Oh, oh. The singing again? Did she never give up?

"Hi, Dad." Jade ran over to greet him.

"Oh hi, honey. You go on out to the car and I'll be right out."

"Okay. Bye, Ms. Davis."

"See you tomorrow, Jade. Good job tonight."

"Thanks."

Judging by the humorous quick glance between them, Jade and Serena both knew she was not completely telling the truth. The rehearsal had been a total bust.

Serena led him over to a corner of the room, probably for privacy again. He geared himself up for what was sure to be another pitch for the pageant.

"No, she can't sing," he said firmly.

"Don't worry. I wasn't going to ask, beg or plead. I wanted to say I'm sorry."

She sounded serious.

"You're sorry? Why? I'm the one who has been rude. It's just I can't let my daughter sing."

"Matt, I never knew about your wife and who she was. I now understand completely why you don't want Jade to sing."

Her eyes looked genuinely concerned and it threw him off. He hadn't expected such compassion, although he knew the Serena he went to school with was kind. She still was.

"Well, thank you. Sometimes I think I am too harsh."

"Maybe. But I get it now."

"Thank you again. I just want to do everything I can to protect my daughter."

"Can't say I blame you. I am sorry about Maya."

"I assumed you knew. For a while there, it seemed like everyone knew and wouldn't leave me alone."

"I didn't, somehow. Immersed in schoolwork, I guess, and not connecting her with you."

"I can see that. She kept her own last name, since she was already known by it. No way would you link Stone with Jenkins."

"She had such a beautiful voice. So heartwarming and sincere."

"She did." He could feel his eyes mist up. "And I'm sorry too for being so blunt the other day."

"No problem. As I said, I do understand."

"Thanks. Well, I'd better get going. Jade's waiting."

"Okay. No problem."

He needed to leave fast before he broke down and made a fool of himself. He'd been on the verge of tears and certainly didn't want to let them loose in front of an audience, no matter how understanding Serena was. In truth, it was her genuine caring that had set him off. He didn't deserve it, especially from someone as sweet as she was.

Practically running to the car, he opened the door and slid in fast.

"Dad, where's your hat?" asked Jade, pulling away her ear pod. "I saw it in your hand back in the church. Did you drop it somewhere?" She giggled. "I barely recognize you without it."

He touched his head. No hat.

Remembering he'd taken it off when he'd entered the church hall, he must have either dropped it or left it on a chair when Serena had approached.

"Guess I forgot it. Be back in a second, honey. I'll just go get it." He hoped he didn't run into Serena again.

"No problem, Dad." After all, she loved listening to music and could probably do so all evening, not even noticing how long he was away.

He hurried in, locating his hat on a chair.

No sign of Serena. She must have left.

He turned to leave when he heard muffled sounds coming from the end of the hall.

Was something wrong?

Curious, he walked over to check it out, realizing the noise seemed to be coming from a room off to the side. He slowly opened the door, identifying the sounds now as music and much to his shock, Serena was dancing. Her eyes were closed, and she looked completely immersed in movement as she swayed and turned, her arms stretching and reaching, her legs leaping and flying. It was obvious she was lost in the music and her beauty literally took his breath away. Something stirred in his heart and he couldn't tear his eyes away. He was mesmerized, overwhelmed by a flood of emotions racing through him, missing the good old days when they had seemed to get along well way back in school. Missing her chattiness, humor and love of life. All before their own disastrous pageant had ended their friendship forever.

Stop it.

No way.

Get a grip.

He couldn't fall for her again. She would never even give him a second glance and he had no time for more heartbreak.

He slipped his hat on and took off fast for the second time.

This was the last thing he needed to deal with.

Love.

Especially unrequited love.

Shock exploded.

Love?

Just what made him think that what he felt was love? It was too intense of a word, let alone a feeling.

Forget about her.

Pronto.

Twelve

A bang on the window sent Holly into a frenzy of excited barking. Serena looked up, grinned, and beckoned Nancy indoors.

"It's okay, Holly. It's a friend, not a foe," she said, soothingly.

"Great watchdog there." Nancy leaned down to pet Holly, who wagged her tail vigorously. "Hey, you know me. Why are you barking?"

Holly jumped up and twirled around as if dancing in delight.

"Showing off now, are you?" Nancy laughed.

"Yes, she is. But when it comes to protecting me, she's on the job constantly. Sorry, I'm beat. Can't get up to greet you. I don't think I can move, even if I want to."

"You do look tired." Nancy walked over to give Serena a brief hug. "Are you sure you're not doing too much? I mean you're teaching full time, giving ballet lessons and baking. I'm surprised you're still upright."

Serena yawned as Holly came back to settle at her feet, having finished her guard bit. Guess realizing she knew Nancy, she felt she could go off duty.

"Well, as you can see, I'm not actually upright." Serena smiled. "I'm more just slumped over. Here..." She leaned over and pulled out a chair. "Grab a seat."

"Where's your mom?" Nancy asked, plopping down on the chair.

"Sent up to rest and eventually go to bed. So happy you dropped by. I just finished with my last ballet student of the day and figured I needed coffee before I faced a round of marking." She gestured to the files on the table. "But having a good friend here makes it all so much better."

"Well, I was out jogging and saw the bakery lights on." Nancy pulled her jacket off and swung it around to hang over the back of her chair. "Figured you were here. Do you ever sleep?"

"About as much as you."

They both laughed.

"Guess we're two of a kind. Always working hard." Nancy glanced over at the stove. "Is your nightly baking at least finished?"

"Mostly. Just have brownies to ice. Can't forget that." Serena yawned again. "Sorry, I'm being rude. But hey, how are you doing?"

"You're not rude and I'm doing fine. Trying to keep the class Christmas spirit from exploding." Nancy's arms flew up into the air mimicking an explosion. "It's lovely most of the time, but if I don't keep control, the little ones will be bouncing off the walls soon."

"I can imagine. It's such an exciting time for children, what with all the big countdowns to Christmas Day."

"All they can think about are presents these days."

Which was exactly why the principal counted on the pageant to remind them of the real meaning of Christmas, thought Serena, noting her friend looked tired, too. She had learned that he was big on prayer, always reflecting on the spiritual side of life in a school.

"Hey, wait a second. Where are my manners? Would you like some coffee?" Serena asked. "A cookie? Cinnamon bun? Would a nice baked good take your mind off school for a while?"

"I hoped you'd offer. I'm always hungry the minute I walk in this door. Oh, don't move. I can get it." She jumped up, grabbed a mug out of the cupboard and headed for the coffeemaker.

"Just like old times. We used to spend hours and hours gabbing away at this very same table."

"And eating cookies and anything else we got our hands on." Nancy giggled. "Mom used to get mad because I'd snack so much here that I never finished supper."

"Yeah, mine, too."

"Oh, I meant to ask you earlier at school, but how's it going with the bakery debt and savings plan?"

"Slow. I'm meeting with the Andersons' real estate agent soon trying to swing a deal."

"Oh, I hope it goes well."

"Me, too."

Nancy sat back down, placing her coffee on the table, cinnamon bun still in her hand. She stared at the big gooey confection.

"I haven't had one of these in ages and I'm going to savor every bite."

Serena chuckled as her friend bit into it, eyes closed, moaning in delight.

"How's the teaching going?" Nancy asked, finally popping open her eyes.

Truth be told, Serena had never taught a class in her life except when practice teaching while at teacher's college. Yes, she was a qualified teacher, but was still studying, working on her doctorate in education, having decided to get as much schooling done now while she was still young. Later could prove more difficult as responsibilities took hold.

"I'm giving it my best," Serena said. "That's all I can say. Trying hard."

Nancy stretched out her legs, getting even more comfortable. "I'm hearing good things about you, by the way."

Serena sat straight up. "Really?"

"Really." Her friend leaned over and squeezed her hand. "From parents. You're getting a good reputation around Angel."

"Nice to know." Serena pushed herself up off the chair and gave her friend a hug. "Thanks for telling me. You just made my day."

"You should know that. As a matter of fact, I ran by, hoping to see you."

"Well, you had perfect timing." Serena pulled away and sat. "I needed a boost tonight."

"Anything I can do to help?"

"Thanks, but you've been such a huge help already, answering all my questions as to how the school operates." Serena sighed. "It's the pageant that's the main issue. For some reason, the kids don't want to do it and I can't seem to inspire them. They'll be good for one practice, or at least for part of it, and then the next one is off the wall."

Nancy popped the last piece of bun in her mouth, chewing slowly.

"Oh, that was good." She moaned in delight.

"Thank my mother. She's the recipe creator. I don't know how she does it. She just seems to know by pure instinct what ingredients go together to enhance the flavor. The icing on top is her own pure invention."

"I love it. Your mom definitely knows how to bake. I'll have to start coming back here more often."

"Well, our special table welcomes you any time. We have a lot to get caught up on."

"Yes, we do. But sorry for switching topics. Now, about the pageant. Seems like students get all caught up in what Santa's going to bring them, even at that age. My kindergarten students are always writing Santa lists, revamping them, adding to them. It's a hectic time. Could you maybe ask the principal to get someone else to direct the play? It's enough that you have to get ready for classes and you don't even have a drama background, do you? Any experience?"

"No. Not at all. I danced for several years and performed in their end of year recitals, but that's it. I've never directed anything." Serena drained the last bit of her coffee. "It is stressful, but I don't feel comfortable asking to be relieved of the pageant. Principal Lemire considers it important and of course I do agree with him that the birth of Jesus is what it's all about. It's just that I have no idea how I'll pull it all off."

"It sounds like an extra burden, especially when you're new and have all those classes to teach." Nancy jumped up. "More coffee?"

"Oh, I can get it."

"No, you just sit there and relax." She picked up the coffee pot and topped up both their mugs. Sitting back down, she continued, "I used to wonder how their regular teacher, Lena Douglas, did it all. Of course, drama was her forte and usually she oversaw re-enacting the Christmas story, since it has always been the seventh grade who performed the pageant. Could you maybe ask her for help?"

"Not really. Comfortably anyway. I called her the other day to ask a few questions about classes and she's busy going through physio. Sounds like she has a lot to deal with, coping with the ACL tear and her own three children." She shrugged, signaling defeat. "Not to mention a husband away a lot on business. I'm lucky to have this job and I want to appear strong and together, hoping I'll get hired after Christmas. Somehow, I've got to figure it all out. And then there is the prop and set situation."

"Oh? What's that about?"

"Well, I assumed that since this pageant was re-created every year, we'd use the old set." Serena rolled her eyes. "Until I discovered there is no old set. Apparently, they take it all apart after Christmas so the new class could be creative and build their own, the goal being fostering community spirit and working together."

She'd had a vague memory of building a set back when she was in the pageant, but it had slipped her mind. Whenever she thought back to those days, what she recalled most was total embarrassment.

"Oh, right. I forgot about that," Nancy said. "But you can always invite the parents in and get it built fast. That's how it's usually done, right? Parents and students working together?"

"Hey, that's a good idea. I forgot about that, because no way can I do it myself. Glad you mentioned it."

"I can help, too."

"Thanks. Have you gotten any better with a hammer?"

"No. You?"

"Not at all."

They burst into laughter.

"It'll be one strange nativity set, that's a given," Serena said. "Especially if we get our hands on it. Remember that treehouse we tried to build in my backyard?" More laughter had them almost falling off their chairs.

"We hammered together two pieces of wood for a platform," Nancy chimed in. "We dragged it up the tree, then realized it blocked us from climbing back down."

"Mom was terrified when a fire engine pulled up in front of the bakery," added Serena, caught up in the merriment. "She rushed to the window and saw two firemen run to the back yard. Guess a neighbor heard our screams."

"They were pretty nice, though. Even helped us lodge the platform safely and built us steps to get there."

"At least it was some place to go, considering I got grounded for a week. I'm just relieved I don't have to make costumes. We apparently reuse them year to year. Guess you can't be too creative there since they're pretty standard. Mary in blue, Joseph in brown, angels in white.

"That's a plus. By the way, how is it going with Matt?" Nancy cocked her head, looking curious. "That's another question I meant to ask earlier on."

"Okay, I guess. We have nothing to do with each other, but during my breaks from teaching and baking today, I scoured the internet for news of his wife. I saw a few photos of them." She reached over and pulled out a few papers from one of the notebooks lying on the table. She slid them over adding, "I'm still shocked and surprised I never knew and that my mother never mentioned it."

"Well, she always has a lot going on." Nancy rifled through the clippings. "It probably slipped her mind."

"You're right. Mom certainly is preoccupied with the bakery and she may not have even remembered him much or the fact I went to school with him. I planned on asking her about it but decided not to bother her."

"Well, if I recall correctly, you had a bit of a crush on him back in the seventh grade." Nancy winked. "Any of those sparks still floating around?"

"With Matt? A crush? Hey, wipe that smile off your face."

"Oh, c'mon. Your face is all flushed. You can't fool me. You know you did."

Serena watched Holly trot over to one of her beds in the dog room. She pretended to be overly interested in her pet, stalling for time. Finally, she answered, "Well, yes. I admit, I did kinda have a crush back then. A little one. Not anymore of course. And no sparks at all now."

Okay, she lied. There were sparks, miniscule ones, but admitting it out loud would only make it worse. It might make her deal with the truth, and that seemed harder than trying to ignore the feelings that popped up here and there. She was too busy to have to face possible romantic feelings.

"Well, what's he like?" Nancy moved her chair closer as if to gather up some juicy gossip. Serena hated to disappoint, but she had nothing to tell. Or at least nothing she wanted to admit.

"He's all right, I guess."

Tucking the photos back in her notebook, Serena was aware of her friend still watching her closely.

"I remember all of us in the Christmas pageant as if it were yesterday," Nancy said.

"Yeah."

"And then you had a big fight. Can't recall all the details, but I know you were upset."

"Well, I was still new and the principal at the time found out I was a dancer. They asked me to perform a ballet number at the end of the drama that night. I was to dance while the singer sang "O Holy Night." It was to enhance the sacredness of the song, or so our teacher said back then." Remembering this was hard. Serena took a deep breath, then continued, "I had only managed to run on stage and get in one plie, when all of a sudden Matt closed the curtain. Bang, it was over. Oh, the song continued but I was done." She could feel her face turn red. "I was so embarrassed and got teased nonstop about that. For some reason, everyone thought I had stage fright and got scared. Or at least that was the gossip going around. I became Serena the scaredy cat ballerina."

"Yeah, I remember. Why did he do it?"

"He said Nick Aldred threw a banana peel on the floor to make me fall, so he pulled the curtain and rushed to get it off the stage. He thought he could reopen it and I could still dance, but the song ended before he finished."

"Oh, right. He protected you."

"No, he didn't. He embarrassed me."

"You didn't believe him?" Nancy looked surprised.

"No. Nick was my friend a lot longer than Matt. Why would he do that? He was both our friends. We trusted him."

"Yes. But you never know. Maybe Matt told the truth. By the way, you know Nick still lives here, right? He's in construction with his brother."

"No, I didn't know. Do you keep in touch?"

"Not at all."

"I seem to recall you had a crush on him."

"I did. Unlike you, I'll admit it." Nancy grinned. "But I was just a kid then. So okay, providing Nick was in the clear, why do you think Matt did it?"

"Not sure. Maybe just a silly prank?"

"So you figure there was no banana peel? Matt just made up that story. Are you sure?"

"Yes. Shutting the curtain had to be intentional. There was no other explanation, and I didn't see any banana peel. I sure got teased, though. It was humiliating."

"Must have been if you haven't forgotten about it all these years."

"Guess I haven't. I was always such a gawky, skinny kid and I didn't like dancing in public, let alone school. I was worried I'd be made fun of, but I caved because I couldn't say no to the principal. And then I was mocked anyway, sparking a nightmare come true."

"Bullying is hard to take."

Serena sighed. "I guess I should let it go. It seems silly to hang on to this all these years. Actually, I hadn't thought about it in ages, but seeing Matt brought it all home again."

"Well, it must have really hurt." Nancy leaned over, taking hold of her hand. "Being teased isn't easy to let go of at any age. But you probably should. At least if you can. Would you consider talking to Matt about it? To clarify facts again? Find out once and for all, from an adult point of view, why he did it?"

"I don't think so. He's probably forgotten all about it."

"Maybe. But think about it anyway."

"I will."

"Promise?"

"Promise."

Nancy looked around. "I sure would hate to see this bakery close. It's a landmark here in Angel."

"Well, I keep hoping it won't."

"Me, too."

"If I get hired on full time as a teacher, I might be able to save it."

"Have you prayed? Miracles can happen, you know."

"A little. I find it hard to ask God to do something special for us when there are so many in need around the world. It just seems so selfish."

"But remember. This is more than just a bakery. It's a place of love and warmth, the calm in the storm, and your mom is a saint."

Serena nodded. "That she is. Somehow I'll have to find a way to make it all work."

"Well, let me know if I can help in any way."

"You already do just by being such a good friend."

"And you never know, dreams still do come true."

Do they? thought Serena. She had difficulty believing that. Especially after her disastrous rehearsals.

"Now, c'mon." Nancy jumped up. "Let me help you ice those brownies. Then you can go straight to marking."

"Thanks. I'd appreciate that and hey, I'll even let you take some home."

"Counting on it."

Feeling refreshed with renewed energy, Serena joined Nancy at the counter. There was nothing like an old friend to brighten her life. She regretted that they had lost touch with one another for a number of years. Yes, she had made new friends at school, but old buddies knew everything about you, every single nuance. It was comforting as well as life-giving, she thought, as she pulled a bowl of icing out of the fridge.

Laughing, reminiscing over old times, discussing their futures, they finished the work in no time at all.

That night as she drifted off to sleep, she had another fervent thought.

She never wanted to lose touch with Nancy again.

True friends were gifts to cherish. Forever.

Thirteen

Matt stood outside Petals, trying to summon up the courage to walk in the door and face Serena. He needed to ask a favor and felt he had no right doing so, especially after not allowing Jade to sing. She may understand, but he didn't think it was enough to allow her to help him in another way.

He'd already walked by the building three times, but could no longer delay. He had to get home soon to make supper for his daughter.

Her words from last night echoed in his head.

"Hey, Dad."

He had looked up to find her standing at the door of his office, looking nervous, swinging back and forth on her feet.

"Yes, honey, come on in."

"Am I bothering you at work?"

"No, of course not. What's on your mind?"

"Well, I've been doing some thinking. If I can't take singing lessons anymore, I wonder if I can take ballet from Ms. Davis."

With Serena? Oh, no.

"Would you like that?"

Her smile had been huge.

"Sure, you know I love to dance."

Yes, he did. Still he had tried to divert her.

"Don't you like helping in the barn with the horses?"

"Well, yeah, but you have good people there. After I take care of Gabrielle, they don't need me and only let me do more stuff because I'm the boss's daughter."

Her smile disappeared and her eyes had darkened with sadness.

"Please. I miss so much of my old life, and dance was a big part of it. I'd love to get back into it."

Instead of saying no right away, he had said, *"Well, let me think about it. We'll see."*

He felt guilty hearing how much she missed her old life, but he should have been prepared for that.

He wasn't.

He'd been in such a rush to get her safe somewhere. And keep her there.

How could he have forgotten that music was such a huge part of her life, and she loved to sing and dance. Well, he knew she loved to sing, but had forgotten about dancing. It was once a huge passion of hers, and he ignored that fact due to his own fear.

It was also his duty to protect her.

His mind swung back and forth between encouraging her to pursue her interests and wanting to hover over her. He wasn't sure what the right answer was, since he was lousy at trying to be both a father and mother to her. If he were graded by a teacher, he'd be an F. A complete failure.

He just felt he had to do something, anything, to make her happy.

Her birthday was a few days away, and he wanted to make it special. Since singing was off the list, maybe signing her up for ballet lessons would be just the thing. Maybe it would bring back the smile on her face she used to have before her mom passed away. Back then she grinned all the time. Not anymore.

He also needed a cake.

Baking was not on his list of culinary skills to date, since the last batch of cupcakes he'd made had risen, then flattened like pancakes. They had to throw them out because they were inedible as well. Something about adding too much salt...and no amount of icing could have saved that disaster.

So here he was at Petals and he had to go into the bakery fast, before he chickened out. Again. The neighboring stores were probably wondering why he walked up and down the sidewalk repeatedly. Could be they'd call the police, deeming him a nuisance. He could just see the headlines. *Local lawyer walks in circles, afraid to face Serena Davis.*

Finally grabbing hold of the doorknob, smiling at his absurd thoughts, he opened the door, walked in, and immediately spotted Serena behind the counter serving customers. Nervous, he picked up a pamphlet off a rack on the wall and sat at one of the tables. He'd wait to ask about the lessons until she was free. Flipping through the small booklet, he checked out the photos of the many cakes available, trying to decide which one to order. They were all incredible, but if the ballet lessons came through, he figured he'd order the ballerina one, full of rich pink and white icing with a tiny dancer perched on top. He knew Jade would love it.

He glanced over to see if Serena had noticed him yet. No, she was still taking orders.

She looked adorable, with that ever-ready smile beaming at everyone.

She was all he could think about lately.

Stop it.

Go back to reading the pamphlet.

He noticed a blurb on the back, explaining the meaning of the name Petals.

Apparently, a rose was Mrs. Davis' favorite flower and she'd penned:

A rose is a beautiful symbol of life and a constant example of how to live and experience growth. We travel up through the stem, working our way through the thorns representing our many challenges, until we emerge blossoming, fragrant, stunning, time and time again. Just like Rose Petals.

Bakeries are like this. We are here to celebrate the happy times such as weddings, birthdays, festive occasions and also to share the sad times such as funerals, disappointments, lack of hope, break-ups. Petals Bakery/Café exists to bring you comfort. Our wish is that it becomes a life-giving/saving oasis where you can drop by at any time, in any state, and be re-energized, and bloom with nurturing petals of hope.

Hence the name, Petals.

Lovely sentiments, thought Matt. No wonder Serena was so kind. Her mother was, and it looked like her daughter was a lot like her. They were quite the team.

"May I help you?"

Startled, Matt looked up and got lost in green eyes.

"Would you like a coffee?" asked Serena, when he didn't answer.

She looked surprised at his mute state. She should be. It was ridiculous.

Stop it. Pay attention.

"Actually, I wonder if you have a few minutes."

She looked around. So did he. No new customers. Good.

"Okay." She sat across from him.

"Well, I, er..." He was nervous, not a condition he was used to. He took a deep breath and began again. "Jade would love to take ballet lessons. I know I don't have the right to ask you. After all, I won't let her sing, but she wants you to teach her. Would you? I'll even pay extra."

"Of course, I will teach her. She's got a natural grace about her and it'd be an honor. And no paying extra, either."

"You will?"

She smiled. "Don't look so surprised. I meant it when I said I understand why you don't want her to sing. She's such a sweet young girl and I'd love to give her dance lessons."

"Do you have time? I know how busy you are."

"I'll make time."

Once again it hit him how nice she was. He wanted to jump up and hug her, anticipating how excited Jade would be, but he felt it would be too forward. Too intimate. It wasn't like they were even friends.

Remember. This is a business deal.

"Well, okay then. Thank you. I appreciate it."

"No problem."

"Oh, and I'd like to order the ballerina cake as well, if that's okay." He pointed to the picture on the brochure.

"Of course, it is. When is her birthday?"

"This weekend. Is it too late to order? Do you need more time? More notice?"

"No, not at all. It's fine."

"And when should I pick it up?"

"You don't. Our policy is to deliver them right to your door."

"Oh, no. I can get it myself. I wouldn't want to bother you."

"Mom's rules. All cakes get delivered. She decided that most people are worn out from party preparations and the last thing they needed to stress about was hurrying over to get the cake. I'll drop it off. I bet you'll have your hands full that day, already. This is just one more item to check off your list of things to do."

He wanted to fight her more on this issue, not wanting to bother her with a cake delivery, but admittedly liked the idea of a visit, even though he tried to avoid her. It didn't make sense, of course, but it seemed to be how his mind worked these days. All over the place, mixed up and confused, but Jade would be thrilled to see her. In truth, so would he.

"Well, okay, then."

She stood up and he immediately felt disappointed. He would have liked to have chatted more, but of course, she had work to do.

"Thank you," he said.

"Would you like some coffee and goodies to go?"

"Yes, please."

"Great. C'mon over and I'll get it ready."

"You don't need my order?"

She grinned. "Cinnamon buns, chocolate chip cookies and coffee, one milk. Correct? Oh, and a hot chocolate for Jade."

"You've got it." He loved seeing her smile, instantly feeling a surge of emotion sweep through him. He quickly looked away, worried he might betray his warm thoughts and blurt something out. Like asking her out on a date, or something. No, he couldn't do that. He needed to keep his feelings hidden away for his own sanity. He had no time for relationships of the romantic kind.

Not that she was interested, anyway.

"Thanks," he muttered.

"No problem."

He followed her over to the serving area.

It took her seconds to put together a bakery box filled with sweets. He pulled out his wallet.

"No, no money. It's on the house."

He started to protest, but noticed she had turned away to greet a group of women walking in the door.

He looked around.

Everyone seemed happy when they were at Petals, and once again he thought how it was such a shame the restaurant was closing. It was a huge loss for Angel.

A tragedy.

Slipping a ten-dollar bill under a coffee cup, he walked out the door to his car.

His mind raced. Was there anything he could do to help save the bakery? He'd have to think about that. Maybe there was.

But for now, he hurried home to be with Jade, hoping she was okay, happy and safe. His heart quickened every time he thought of her.

He just couldn't lose her too.

Fourteen

"Are you sure you want to come in with me, Mom?" Serena asked, as she pulled into a parking spot and shut off the motor.

"Yes, dear. You shouldn't have to face this alone. After all, it's really my problem, not yours."

"Well, okay, then. I wanted to spare you." She jumped out, ran around and opened the door for her mother. "Just remember, your name may be on the lease, but we're in this together. It's not just your problem. I'm going to help in any way possible."

"That's lovely dear, but I still feel awful that you're not in school."

"Don't. It's exactly the way I want it. After all, I was going to end up teaching anyway. I'm just doing it earlier."

"You've given up on your doctorate?"

"No, I'll keep plugging away at it part-time. Anyway, it's best to get experience first-hand in the classroom and I find I'm loving it."

In fact, she was surprised at how much she enjoyed it. Overseeing the pageant, not so much, but teaching was exciting. Maybe it was a cliché but opening the doors of learning to young people was rewarding, stimulating, exhilarating. She loved the challenge of making subjects interesting and, as that old saying went, thinking outside the box and being creative when teaching her students. Now, if only she could do that with the pageant. That was where she really needed dramatic skills which she sadly lacked. For now, she was failing, but she'd certainly keep on trying. She had no choice. She simply had to pull it off and do a good job. So much was riding on its success.

"Well, here we are," Mary said, standing still, staring up at the real estate office.

"Yes, here we are."

As they walked up the stairs, Serena checked out her mother. She was no longer wearing her boot cast, not using a cane, and well on the road to a complete recovery. Serena was proud of her and all the exercises and hard work she had done to help herself heal, for she walked up the steps like a pro. A true inspiration.

Finally, arriving at the door, Serena sucked in a deep breath and blew it out, searching for courage. She needed to keep focused. Throwing her shoulders back, she pulled open the door, and together they walked into the foyer of the office. Time to negotiate or even beg. Her mother couldn't lose her bakery. She just couldn't.

Serena paused a moment to send up a prayer.

Lord, I know you care about my mother's café. You care about everything pertaining to everyone. Please let it not be sold to someone else. Please help us save it. Please. Remember, it's not just a place of eating, but a place of good will. My mother's way of serving You.

"Are you okay?" her mother whispered.

"Yes, just praying."

"Good. Me, too. But we don't want to be late."

"You're right."

Their appointment was with a Mr. Johnson. Spotting a sign with his name on it, they walked over to his cubicle. Usually, her mother knew everyone in town, but she had already explained he was new and she'd never met him.

Serena peeked her head around an open space. It was just a small area surrounded by partitions sectioning off offices. "Excuse me, sir, I'm Serena Davis. Are you ready for us?"

A young man looked up from papers he appeared to be poring over. "Oh, hello. Come on in." He smiled as he stood.

"And this is my mother, Mary Davis."

"Nice to meet you," he said, shaking their hands. "Please, take a seat, and call me Harry."

"Thank you," Mary said.

They sat, Serena drawing in another deep breath and letting it out. She needed to be attentive and alert. Focused.

"So how can I help you?" he asked, sitting back, hands clasped on the desk.

"It's about Petals," her mother said.

"Yes, the bakery. Great muffins, by the way. Our receptionist bought some the other day, and I'm afraid I ate three of them."

"Well, thank you. I'm glad you enjoyed them. I am the owner and my daughter is helping me."

"Yes, I am aware of that. Glad to meet you both." His tone had changed. He now sounded clipped and stern. Not a good start.

"Well..." Her mother faltered. Serena glanced over and noted she was close to tears. Couldn't blame her. Petals was her world, her creation, and Mr. Johnson certainly wasn't the friendliest. In all fairness to him, though, he probably had guessed why they were there and possibly felt uncomfortable, knowing he'd have to turn them down.

"We want to buy the building," Serena said, jumping right in. Might as well get to the point. "Please tell us it's not sold yet."

He shook his head.

"It's not sold yet. At least, the deal is not complete. I do have an interested and credible buyer. My understanding is that you, and I'm sorry to be so blunt, can't afford it. As you probably know, the owner is retiring, has left town and wants to sell it pronto. A buyer has approached me with a verbal commitment and he's flying here in the new year to sign papers."

"The sale is not officially completed yet?" asked her mother. "I thought it was. But nothing's been actually formalized?"

Serena could hear the longing in her mother's voice. Even though she had suggested it was time to retire, it was obvious she didn't want to. Makes sense, since baking was her life and she loved every minute of it.

"Correct. Not yet. But to be honest, soon. It's practically a done deal."

Good news, though. Nothing official, for at least a few more weeks.

"Could you give us until January first?" Serena asked. "To possibly buy it ourselves? We're trying to round up the money. Would Mr. Anderson agree to do that?"

Although he lived in another city, she'd met the owner a few times at the bakery. He seemed pleasant. Maybe, just maybe, he'd agree to wait to see if they could gather the money themselves.

Harry hemmed and hawed. "Well, it won't hurt for me to give Mr. Anderson a call and ask. After all, he did offer the building to you first."

"Would you do that?" her mother asked. "Please?"

"Now?" added Serena.

He locked eyes with her mother and Serena was sure he'd say no.

"Well, okay," he finally said.

Guess he couldn't resist the pleading in her mom's eyes. Also, the sadness.

He picked up his phone, hit buttons, chatted a few minutes, and hung up.

"Okay. Mr. Anderson, who is a great fan of yours, by the way, will hold off signing the deal until we have first heard from you in the new year. Will that work?"

"Yes. Thank you so much," Mary gushed.

Serena added her own heartfelt thanks.

"The whole town respects you, Ms. Davis," Harry said. "Your daughter as well. I wish you all the best and hope things work out for you."

"Thank you again," Serena said. "We appreciate your help."

So, he wasn't so bad after all. A good lesson in not judging too quickly.

After saying goodbye, they headed to their next stop, the bank, two doors down.

"I know you want to try for a loan, but this will be fruitless," her mother said, as they walked down the sidewalk. "I've already gone this route."

"I know, but another attempt won't hurt."

A loud voice bellowed out, "Hey there. Is that you, Serena?"

What?

She turned to see who had addressed her. A young man in heavy construction wear was standing there smiling.

"Do I know you?"

He pulled off his hat and sunglasses. She stared.

"Nick Aldred? Is that really you?"

"Yes. I heard you were in town. I planned on stopped by the bakery to say hello but just hadn't gotten around to it yet."

"Well, please do. Anytime."

"How are you doing?"

"Great. And you?"

"Can't complain." His phone buzzed and he pulled it out of his pocket to glance at the screen. "Sorry, I can't talk any longer. Gotta run. Just heading into work and there's already a problem. I'll see you later. I'll grab some coffee at the bakery soon."

"Looking forward to it. Take care."

All she could think of was, *did he leave a banana peel on the stage all those years ago?* Or was Matt lying? Odd how she had been so quick to believe Nick way back then. Was she wrong?

She shook her head, struggling to clear it. Amazing it still bothered her after all these years. Then again, she was back in the midst of old memories and present day contact with the same individuals, so she couldn't help herself.

Enough.

She had serious work to do.

She hurried to catch up to her mother, who had continued on, probably giving them privacy, or was so locked in her own worries she hadn't noticed Serena wasn't beside her.

"Who was that, dear? An old friend?"

Guess her mom was just giving her space.

"Nick Aldred."

"Oh, right. He's a contractor."

"So I've heard."

"A good one, too. He did some work on the kitchen for me a while back. Didn't recognize him all bundled up."

"Oh. I never knew he worked for you." She wanted to ask more, but they were at their destination, so she dropped it.

Serena prayed again as they walked in and were ushered right to the loan clerk's office by a sweet girl with a receptionist tag pinned to her sweater. She appeared good at her job, and her smile was calming and reassuring. The officer herself was a tall, lean, grey-haired woman who sported a huge smile.

"Hello, Mary," the woman said. "And this is your lovely daughter, Serena, I take it?"

"Yes," her mother answered.

"I'm Selma Jones." She reached out her hand for a shake.

"Pleased to meet you." Serena hoped the woman's friendliness was a sign of good things to come. Although Harry had been that way at the beginning...

After another round of handshakes, Ms. Jones gestured to a grouping of chairs. "Please, take a seat." She settled herself behind her desk. "Now, what can I do for you?"

"Well," Serena said, sitting, leaning forward. "I wonder if you would consider loaning us the money to buy the building housing the bakery."

"Oh, I'm sorry." Ms. Jones looked genuinely upset. "Your mother and I have already discussed this. I can't help you. I wish I could because I enjoy Petals and have spent plenty of time there over the years."

"But what if I get a full-time job at the school?" asked Serena. "And we worked out a payment plan."

Silence. Ms. Jones looked thoughtful as she drummed her fingers on the desk.

"Well. It certainly would change matters. Are you hired full time?"

"Not yet. I'm there temporarily."

"Oh, right. I did hear that a new teacher was covering Lena's classes and the pageant. Is that you?"

Serena almost didn't want to admit it. She had no trouble acknowledging she was teaching, but when it came to the pageant, she was convinced it would bomb. It also meant she'd never be hired full time. But she needed to show confidence.

"Yes, it's me. They are also looking to hire someone permanently in the new year. One of their teachers is retiring."

"Hmmmm…" Ms. Jones looked deep in thought. "Well, come back when you are hired. We probably can figure out an arrangement then."

Probably? Serena's heart sung. She could handle a probably.

Once more, she crossed her fingers and uttered a prayer.

Please, God. Please let this pageant go well.

Fifteen

It was all Matt could do to stop himself from telling Jacob/Joseph off. Last night at dinner, Jade declared he was a silly boy, a jokester, but didn't mean any real harm and was quite nice. Matt disagreed. Once again, Jacob's ridiculous antics had turned the pageant into something trivial, a laughing matter, rather than a sacred tribute to the birth of Christ.

It wasn't funny anymore. Didn't even warrant a small smile.

Not wanting to interfere in Serena's turf, he kept quiet.

Continuing his habit of arriving early to pick up Jade, he strived to be a support for his daughter, or at least that was what he told himself. In truth, he wanted to see Serena as well. Just couldn't stop himself, even though he was still conflicted, wanting to stay away from her, yet seeking her out at the same time. He felt like a teenager all over again.

Today, however, was a special treat for the class.

Serena had permission from all the parents to meet her students at Petals after rehearsal for hot chocolate and goodies. He'd forgotten about it, immersed in legal briefs, or else he would have arrived later, picking up his daughter there, instead. Considering he was already at the church hall, he decided to go as well, albeit sit at another table, and as the rehearsal came to an end, he made his way to the bakery, trailing behind the group.

Walking in the door, savoring the blended smells of vanilla, cinnamon and hot chocolate, he bought a coffee and a cookie, then pulled up a chair at a nearby table. Serena had her back to him so she didn't see him. He looked around, still enjoying the beautiful warmth of the bakery with its Christmas decorations, and sad once again that this wonderful little café was soon closing. As time went on, he had learned it really was the hub of the town where people gathered for every occasion and Serena's mother, from what he heard and understood, was an incredibly sweet person, not to mention overly generous. He watched her bring plates of gingerbread to the table while Serena poured hot drinks for the class. Mrs. Davis' beautiful smile was the mirror image of her daughter's and her loveliness had been passed down. Her eyes looked worried, though, underlined by dark smudge marks, and she appeared tired. He wished he could reduce her stress.

"Mom, where is your favorite nutcracker?" Serena asked, surprise in her voice. "The gold one you love so much."

Matt shouldn't be listening, but couldn't help it. After all, she said this in front of the students, not that they showed any interest, for they were too busy gobbling down cookies, so it wasn't as if he were eavesdropping. And from the looks of it, her mother collected nutcrackers.

"Oh, I sold it, honey." Mary turned away fast.

"But you love that particular one." Serena moved to stand in front of her. "What's going on? You searched hard for a gold one and finally found it at that little tea place we went to when you visited me last summer."

"Yes, well, a customer offered me quite a lot of money for it and every little bit helps."

Serena gave her a quick hug. "Yes, you're right, I guess. But I know how much you particularly loved the shiny color of that one."

"It's okay, dear," her mother said, pulling away, patting her daughter's shoulder, then walking back to the kitchen.

Matt watched as Serena distributed napkins and at one point, he could see her face and noticed she looked disappointed, upset, or maybe just sad. Not happy, for sure. She sat and said to the class, "The reason I wanted to come here is because we all need to talk."

She sounded dead serious. Hmmm... so this was more than a drinking chocolate and eating cookies treat.

"What about?" Julie asked.

"Yeah, sorry I dropped the doll again," Jacob said, sounding guilty. "It just slipped."

Matt frowned. No matter how many times that boy was asked to stop, he always managed to let the doll fall, as if on cue. If it were scripted, it'd be perfect, but it upset him to see Serena patiently try to constantly explain how they needed to take the pageant seriously. Not to mention it bothered the rest of the cast, who had gone from giggling over the prank to now being annoyed. A few still laughed, but not as many and once again, he felt like yelling at the boy to tell him to smarten up.

"Well, I thought we should chat about what you feel is the true meaning of Christmas," Serena said, cutting into his thoughts.

Most looked surprised. Guess they'd expected a lecture. Others were still concentrating on their hot chocolate and goodies, eyes down.

No one said a word.

"Anyone want to go first?" Serena asked. "Please?"

"Well..." Julie said. "It's about presents, I guess. Presents we get and ones we give."

Serena leaned forward, looking excited. Probably happy a student was finally speaking up. "Yes. Presents were also first given by shepherds and wise men to honor the child Jesus."

"My mom says it's about being kind." Jacob grinned, looking quite proud of himself. "That we should be nice all the time, but Christmas makes us think about it more. And we should do something about it."

Matt was surprised Jacob had come up with that. Too bad he didn't apply it to his own life, although his daughter said he did. Apparently, he was especially good with the kindergarten class during lunchtime, making sure they could open their juice boxes successfully. He then helped them with their coats and boots and spotted them on jungle gyms out in the yard, preventing them from falling. Matt wished his kindness would spill over to the pageant.

"True," Serena said. "Good point."

"Kind!" Julie glared at Jacob. "Yeah, right. Then why are you so mean to that doll? I'm still scared you'll drop my baby brother when we do it for real."

Matt smiled. She said exactly what he was thinking.

"I won't. I promise. It's just that the doll's so light I keep forgetting I'm holding it."

"Let's keep focused," Serena said. "We're talking about the real meaning of Christmas."

Julie rolled her eyes, but dropped it.

"Anyone else have something to add?" Serena looked around the table.

Matt watched Jade look up, as if thinking.

Then she spoke.

"It's all about love," she said softly.

His breath caught in his throat as he leaned forward to listen.

"Yes?" Serena asked, encouragingly. "What about love, Jade?"

"Well..." She put down her hot chocolate. "My mom always said it's a huge celebration of joy and good will. She used to talk about that first Christmas a lot, where there were probably no decorations and if there were any, they'd be made of straw and wood and the only guests at first were cows, donkeys, and sheep. Nothing too showy or anything. Nobody had much and all that was important was the love between Mary, Jesus, and Joseph." She smiled. "Mom said, like Julie and Jacob did, that we should give presents to others, too, especially those in need, out of love, because that's what Jesus would do. And that's what God would like us to do."

She was obviously remembering happy times, Matt thought.

Silence ensued.

Jade's voice was so incredibly soft, so moving, it seemed to stop everyone literally in their tracks. Not a word was spoken for a few seconds.

Matt wiped away a tear.

"Jade, thank you for sharing that." Serena nodded. "What you said is beautiful."

"And you know what else?" Jade burst out excitedly. "My mom had a secret. A big, big secret. Something she did every Christmas, and something I still do."

She did? Matt was surprised. And Jade still does it?

It was news to him.

"And she only told me," Jade continued. "Because we did it together."

"What is it?" Julie asked.

Jade shook her head. "Can't tell. I got excited and guess I spoke too soon. I probably shouldn't have mentioned it."

"You have to now," Jacob said.

"No, you don't, Jade," said Serena. "Not if you don't want to."

"Please tell us," Julie begged. "Please."

Matt watched Jade look around at all her classmates, then suddenly spotted him.

Oh, oh. He wondered if she would be angry.

She looked surprised, then smiled.

Good.

He smiled back.

Her eyebrows rose and he instinctively felt she was asking him what to do.

He nodded and mouthed *go ahead*. He wanted to know the answer, too.

She briefly tilted her head towards him, then turned to her classmates. "Well, I guess I can tell, because the more people who do it, the better this world will be. I'm sure my mom would like to spread it all around. And some of you are probably doing this anyway."

"What is it?" asked Jacob, sounding impatient.

Matt looked at all the children who appeared mesmerized. He was, too.

Jade spoke slowly.

"Well, my mom called it heart gifts. It's very simple. It's gifts of kindness from the heart. Every Christmas, my mom did one thing for someone and no one knew. It was a secret. She said it was between her and God, to honor the baby Jesus through taking care of someone in need. I do that as well."

Matt had no idea.

"Like what?" asked Julie.

"Well." Jade leaned in, an excited look on her face. "You keep your eyes open for someone who needs something or who is sad or lonely. And you try to help, but you don't let them know what you're doing. You silently give them a heart gift. Only Mom and I knew. And, of course, God."

"Really?" Julie looked puzzled. "What did you actually do? Like, how exactly did you help? Any examples?"

"Yeah. Tell us more," Jacob added.

"Well, like one time we left diapers outside the door of a single mom who we discovered didn't have much money and was struggling to keep afloat. We also left a huge box of mitts and sweaters at a park where we knew some homeless people lived." Jade's voice rose in excitement. "And once I slipped some money into the pocket of a coat of someone who I overheard say they had lost their job. I worked the coat check that night at church, so it was easy to do. Another time, we sat all morning in our car, waiting for a family to leave, so we could drop off Christmas presents on their porch. Mom found out the dad was sick and needed expensive medication and they had nothing left for gifts. We kept it all quiet."

"Did they ever find out anyway and thank you?" Jacob asked.

"No, never. We were quick and secretive, and they never knew who did it. Only we did. We didn't want or need recognition or thanks. Mom always said we were trying to share God's love and doing what He would want done. Being his eyes, arms and legs, so to speak."

Silence reigned around the table, as everyone looked deep in thought.

To Matt's surprise, once again his eyes flooded with tears. Yes, his wife was deeply compassionate and kind, and she had obviously passed this down to Jade. How sad that he didn't even know they had done this. The realization also hit that he had denied her another partner in all of it, caught up in his own indifference with God and himself. Simply not paying attention to anything but his own fear.

He needed to stop.

To ask forgiveness.

From Jade, from God, from himself.

At least for the sake of his daughter.

He looked around at the students. Jade's enthusiasm touched them in a way even Serena couldn't. She truly was a special person, this daughter of his, and he needed to remember that. He felt in awe of her at the moment.

"You made a lot of lovely points, Jade," Serena said. "An act of kindness done in secret is such a wonderful idea."

"Heart gifts," Julie said. "I like that."

"Me, too." Jacob nodded his head vigorously.

"So, let's all do it." Julie stood, snapping her fingers.

To Matt's surprise, the whole class applauded.

Jade looked excited.

"Are you serious?"

"Yes," Jacob said.

"I'd love that. I miss doing this with my mom." The biggest grin ever appeared on Jade's face. "We used to spend hours searching for people who needed help and then feeling so happy that we could make them smile for a minute or two."

Too bad she couldn't have shared this with me, thought Matt once again. But then again, when his wife was alive, he was rarely home.

"Since the name of our school is Angel," Julie said, sitting again. "How about we call it Angel Heart Gifts. Would that work?"

"I like it." Jade gave her the thumbs up.

Matt noticed that Serena was beaming. "What a great idea," she added, "And thank you, Jade, for sharing this."

Jade's eyes glowed. Matt's heart exploded with love at how happy she appeared. The first time in a long time.

"So, Operation Angel Heart Gifts officially begins right now," Julie said. "All who agree, raise your hands."

Every single student had their hand in the air. He was so proud of Jade he wanted to run right over and hug her. Of course, he didn't, not wanting to embarrass her.

"Hey, about being kind and giving, guess we're making a huge mess of the pageant, aren't we?" Jacob asked. "Especially me. I keep dropping the baby Jesus all the time, and Jade is right. He represents love. I'm ashamed of myself."

"Me, too," spoke up one of the shepherds. "We don't take it very seriously."

Everyone nodded.

He watched Serena smile and instantly understood what she was attempting to do. She wanted the students to understand the real meaning of Christmas, which would impact on their acting. Smart strategy, if it worked, for it would be coming from them, not from an authority figure and therefore more effective. Peer pressure at its best.

"We need to be better," Julie said. "And I have an idea. Er, can we run through it again, this time more serious and not goof around?"

"In the café?" asked Jacob. He looked around doubtfully. "Maybe we could go back to the school."

Somehow these two seemed to be the voice of the class, or the ones with the loudest voices. Matt vaguely remembered that Jade had said they were both on the student council and represented the class. Often, he saw other students whisper things to them. Guess they were the chosen spokespeople, which was excellent, because if they were all for heart gifts, it would go well. The same with the pageant. They seemed determined now to make it work. Good. He hoped they would try harder.

"No, we can't." Julie shook her head. "My parents are picking me up here. It's the same with most of us."

"There is space over there." Serena pointed to a corner of the room. She had jumped on board, moving with her students' initiative. Smart move. "It's tight, but we could just go through it without props, focusing on the words and actions with more meaning. Everyone in agreement?"

A chorus of yeses rang out.

"How about we start with a prayer first. Jade, would you like to lead us?"

His daughter looked startled.

"Oh, no, maybe someone else should." She turned red.

Guess she wasn't ready for that yet, thought Matt.

"I will," Jacob said.

"Okay." Serena looked surprised. "Go ahead."

"Dear God, I'm sorry I keep dropping the baby Jesus. Yes, it's a doll, but it represents You and I feel bad about this now. Help me to stop doing this and please help us to do a good job of the pageant for a change. Let's all try hard. And bless our Angel Heart Gifts. Guide us so that we can find people who need us. Amen."

Matt couldn't help but smile. Maybe Jacob really was the nice guy Jade kept saying he was. As that old saying goes, time would certainly tell.

"Very good," Serena said. "Now let's run through the play one more time. Concentrate hard on what you are saying and acting out. We are trying to bring the baby Jesus alive to everyone."

Matt watched her hurry over and tell her mother what they were doing. Mary nodded in agreement, said a few words, then pulled something off a shelf. It was a bag of sugar. She handed it to Serena. He wondered what that was all about.

"Here, Jacob." Serena hurried over to give him the bag. "This sugar represents the baby Jesus."

Matt chuckled. If he dropped it, he'd be in big trouble.

Jacob took hold of the sugar, cradling it in his arms, looking at it almost tenderly.

"Don't let it fall," Julie said, "cuz you'll make a real mess."

"I won't."

Matt wasn't convinced.

"Okay, everyone. We need to try harder," Julie said. "Let's surprise Ms. Davis."

And they did.

They ran through their lines and movements with hardly any errors, or none he could see. Jacob never dropped the sugar bag even once. The focus on their faces showed real commitment.

As they neared the end, the time arrived for the song "O Holy Night." Surprisingly, Jade volunteered to sing. As her notes soared into the air, everyone stared at her, enthralled.

Maybe he should let her sing.

No, keep focused.

You need to protect her.

When the song was over, everyone cheered and Matt stood up, accidentally scraping the chair against the floor.

Was it an accident? Or was he trying to cut into the interest focused on his daughter, not liking it. Or simply wanting Serena's attention.

She turned around and gasped, not realizing he was there. She walked over just as his heart started beating fast. He wanted to talk to her, but didn't, all at once. Same old dilemma. He felt like one of her students, hoping he hadn't let her down.

"Your daughter is amazing," she said.

"Thank you. I think so, too, but I'm biased."

"Did you hear what she talked about tonight?"

He nodded.

"Funny how you're so angry with God, and she's so in love with God. Her eyes lit up when she shared."

Yes, they did.

Leave it to Serena to speak the truth.

He hung his head, ashamed.

Sixteen

It was Friday, Jade's birthday.

Serena had been overjoyed to see how excited she was when the whole class sang "Happy Birthday" to her and presented a cake, covered with candles, made by, of all people, Jacob. The girl positively glowed and it was obvious she had made a ton of friends and was nicely settling in her new school.

Serena, however, didn't want to see Matt. Every time she did, he stirred up emotions buried for years. Ones she didn't want to face.

Now why did she have to go and offer to drop off that cake?

He'd wanted to pick it up, so she should have just let him. She could have arranged to be in the back room when he did. Out of eye and ear shot.

No, she couldn't.

It was true. Her mom insisted cakes be hand-delivered. Another thoughtful gesture she did for everyone in town, always thinking of others first. And here her daughter was thinking only of herself.

Get it together.

This was about a young girl's birthday cake and the joy it would bring her. Not about her mixed feelings about Matt.

Glancing at her watch, she realized she had quite a bit of time before her delivery and all her marking was done, as well as all baking completed. She didn't need to arrive at the Jenkins house until later, so she hurried back to the dog room.

"C'mon, Holly and Gloria. Let's go for a walk."

The two dogs wagged their tails, equally excited about going out and about on an adventure. She was, too. She needed some quality time in fresh air to get her thoughts in order.

Pulling on her winter coat and boots, bundling up for the cooler weather, she snapped leashes on the dogs and went out the back. She turned onto the main street to head through town.

"Hi, Margaret."

"Hi, Sarah."

"Hi, Fred."

Serena was amazed at how many people she knew now, as she greeted folks walking along the sidewalks, shopping, drinking coffee and hanging out. Taking deep breaths of the glorious fresh air, she looked around at all the brightly painted shops lining the street, all dressed up and ready for Christmas. Angel was an imaginative and special place to live, and she had missed it. She was glad to be back.

"Is it true the bakery is going to be sold?" Jim asked. He ran the local butcher shop and was out shoveling snow off the sidewalk.

"Yes," Serena said. "Still hoping for a miracle."

"It's our heart," his wife called out, poking her head out the door. "Our favorite place in the world."

"Mine, too. Thanks for your kind words." Serena was touched. "My mother and I appreciate them."

She hadn't realized how many would miss Petals, which made her feel even more anxious to save it. She had to keep trying and think positive. Also pray. That was key. It was going right to the top to ask for guidance, help, and the strength to keep fighting. She still hoped to discover strategies that might help.

Circling around the town, enjoying the sights and camaraderie, she finally arrived at the bakery and scooted down the alleyway to the back door again.

"Did you have a nice walk, dear?" Mary asked, reaching to take Gloria's leash as she walked in.

"Yes, and I think your dog will sleep for a while now. But I'm taking Holly out again."

Holly howled in delight, understanding the world 'out' and realizing her leash was still intact, which meant she was going somewhere else.

"Hey, is that Holly I hear?"

Serena glanced up to see who emerged into the kitchen from the bakery.

"Sunny?" She glanced at the apron she was wearing, recognizing the Petals' rose motif. "You're working here?"

"She popped in earlier while you were out walking, wanting to volunteer," her mother said. "Isn't that amazing? So, I put her right to work."

"My doctor gave me the okay." Sunny leaned over to pat Holly on the head. "And since my classes are mainly in the afternoon, I thought I'd help out here. You and your mom have always been so kind to me, it's time I give back."

Serena's eyes filled with tears. They could use an extra pair of hands, which would lighten the load, especially for her mother and Helen.

"Thank you." She clasped the young girl in a hug. "You're an angel."

"Well, it's my pleasure," Sunny said. "And hey, I have your cake all boxed up and ready to go, but you ought to look at it. Your mother outdid herself."

Serena pulled away and walked over to the counter to lift the lid up and take a peek. It was larger than her normal cakes, and stunningly beautiful with soft swirls of pink and white icing highlighting a ballerina practicing at the bar. A bar created with pretzels and licorice. The tiny doll had blonde hair, just like Jade's, tied back in an elegant chignon. Original, exciting, and gorgeous.

"Wow. Thanks, Mom. You really did go all out today."

"Just wanted to make it special for that poor girl with no mother."

"Well, you did just that."

Her mom had the biggest heart ever. Tears slid down her cheek as she loaded up the cake in the van, added Holly, and headed to Matt's. Mary was definitely her main inspiration in life and a reminder to always think of others. Something she often failed at. Especially this morning when she was regretting the fact she had to take the cake to Matt's.

"Right, Holly? My mom's amazing."

Serena laughed as Holly barked, agreeing with her. After all, her mom let her out every morning to play with Gloria, which was a huge bonus for her fur friend.

"You're my inspiration, too," she added. "You're always so joyful and in love with life that you remind me to work some playtime into my own schedule. But you must behave today. No carrying on or stealing food or snuggling up to Matt. We'll make it quick and skedaddle fast."

Serena glanced in the back mirror, smiling at Holly looking so angelic. With those huge puppy eyes and tufts of hair sticking up all over, she was adorable.

"Yeah, I know that look. Innocent on the outside, but total trouble on the inside."

Holly barked again.

"Definitely agreeing, are you?"

Pulling into the Jenkins laneway, she noticed the whole house was lit up as if there were bright candles in every room. She parked, leashed Holly again and carefully walked up to the door, leading her dog with one hand and holding the cake with the other. Quite the balancing act, but it seemed to work.

She rang the doorbell.

Matt opened the door immediately, as if watching for her.

Oh, why did he have to wear that green plaid shirt and jeans?

Her heart skipped a beat as she registered how good he looked. Breathtaking, actually. And why didn't his hair stay put instead of always drooping over his forehead? Once again, it was all she could do to keep from reaching up to brush it back in place. Thank goodness her hands were tied up with the cake and Holly.

"Hey, thanks for dropping this off." He took the cake from her. "Come on in. It's pretty cold out."

Was it? She found it hot, burning hot. Probably from embarrassment over where her thoughts were headed.

"Sorry, can't, I'd better get going."

"At least say hello to Jade. She'd love to see you."

Guess it was rude not to speak to the guest of honor. "All right."

She stepped into the foyer, closing the door behind her. Once again, Holly whined, barked, then put her paws up on Matt's knees.

"Get down, Holly. You know you're not supposed to jump up."

She ignored Serena, completely besotted with Matt. Again.

"Oh, I don't mind. She's just being friendly." He placed the cake on a table in the hallway and pulled her up into his arms, accepting her sloppy kisses.

It only endeared him more to Serena. As usual.

"Could you not stay a while?" he asked.

"Oh, no, I have a lot to do. I'll just say hello to the birthday girl and leave."

As if on cue, Jade came running out into the hall. "Hi, Ms. Davis. Please stay. Please."

Obviously, she had overheard Matt, but she looked and sounded excited.

"I can't."

"Please, please, I want you to meet someone." She did the whole pout look. Exaggerated but adorable. "Please?"

"Oh, well, okay." How could she say no to such a sweet girl? And that pout was well-done.

Shrugging out of her coat and boots, she followed Jade into the living room. Matt came too, still holding Holly, managing to carry the cake as well. Serena looked around.

It was a very warm and inviting room with dark brown couches sporting sky blue throws scattered about. A tan-colored easy chair was nestled under a hanging lamp; a small table holding a pile of books sat nearby. Obviously, a cozy little reading nook. The whole room was painted a calming forest green, photos on the walls depicted various nature scenes, and a fire snapped and crackled in the woodstove, inviting you to curl up and enjoy. It was also beautifully decorated for a party, with pink and white streamers and balloons, in keeping with the color scheme of the cake. But where were the guests? She looked around. She had expected to see other students there. Instead, it was just Jade and her father. That seemed rather surprising.

"Look." Jade pointed to a small green dog bed off to the side and fast asleep inside of it was a tiny pup.

"I'd like you to meet Ivy," Jade said. "She's nine weeks old and a golden retriever."

Serena moved closer to take a look. "She's adorable."

Holly eased out of Matt's arms, squirming to be let down. He placed her carefully on the floor and she trotted over.

"Be careful, Holly. She's very small."

Her dog hovered over the sleeping pup, then sat and just watched her. Seemed like she had found a new love.

"Be right back." Matt disappeared out the doorway with the cake.

"I call her Ivy," Jade said. "Because I love Christmas too, like you. The holly and the ivy—get it?"

"Sure do."

"Daddy gave me her as a birthday gift, along with ballet lessons. You're going to be my teacher, right?"

"Yes, I am. I'm looking forward to it."

"Me, too."

Matt came back into the room.

"Would you stay for a piece of cake?" he asked.

"Please," Jade begged.

"Well, okay. Just a small one, though." She was still surprised there were no other people there. Not even Matt's sister.

He left again, presumably to get the cake ready.

"Do you need any help, Matt?" she yelled in the direction of the doorway.

"No, I'm good."

Meanwhile Ivy woke up, yawned and stood, surveying her new home. Holly moved closer to inspect her, giving her a little lick, then sat again, continuing to keep vigil. Serena was glad she was being very careful with the pup.

"Oh, look. Ivy likes Holly." Jade clapped her hands. "Good. I wanted them to be friends."

Guess Ivy did, for the pup eventually stumbled out of her bed and cuddled up against Holly.

Jade sat on the floor and Serena joined her as they took turns petting the wee dog and letting her wander around, getting to know her surroundings. Holly instantly became her guard as she trailed behind her everywhere she went.

"Happy birthday to you."

Serena looked up to see Matt singing away as he brought in the cake loaded with candles. She joined in, while Jade jumped up and raved about how lovely the decorations were.

"Now make a wish and blow out the candles," Matt said.

She did, looking starry-eyed. Serena wondered what she wanted, but whatever it was, it seemed to make her happy just thinking about it. She had a huge smile on her face the whole time.

"Come on out to the kitchen," Matt said. "I have plates, forks and hot chocolate awaiting."

Serena followed while Jade stayed behind to try and catch Ivy, who was exploring under the couch.

The kitchen was stunning.

Serena looked around, marveling at its beauty. It was spacious, painted pale yellow, and numerous photos of glorious sunrises stretched across the walls. A large wooden island sat in the middle where Matt was cutting the cake.

"Would you mind grabbing the ice cream out of the freezer, honey?" asked Matt.

"I can do that." Serena laughed.

Matt looked around, startled. "Oh, sorry. Thought you were my daughter."

"No, she's collecting the dogs." She reached into the freezer. "But here's the ice cream." She placed the carton beside the cake, opening it up.

"Thanks."

She watched as he slid a piece of cake on each plate; she picked up the scoop and added a dollop of ice cream, enjoying the quiet camaraderie.

When they were finished, he shouted, "Jade. Can you please come into the kitchen?"

"I'm here, Dad." She walked in holding Ivy. Holly pranced at her feet, and when she noticed Matt, ran right over to him. He scooped her up and she licked his face. Guess he was still the love of her life.

After a brief prayer, they sat around the table eating, Jade held Ivy while Matt had Holly on his lap. Humorously, Serena wished her mom's dog were there so she'd have her own pet to mind as well.

"Soooo good," Jade said, taking the last bite of her cake. She was clearly in a great mood, as she began chatting about other birthdays she'd had and how this one was even more special because of Ivy.

"I've always wanted a dog." Jade snuggled her new pet a little closer. "And this farm will be a great home, because there's lots of land for Ivy to run around on."

"She'll love it," Serena said. "Plenty of new smells to explore, too. Sometimes I call my walks 'sniffs' because that's all Holly wants to do."

Jade laughed. "Speaking of sniffing, I'm going to take her out later to meet Gabrielle. She'll have to get used to horses."

"Great idea." Matt nodded. "The faster we adapt her to her new surroundings, the more comfortable she'll feel."

Serena relaxed and found she enjoyed the excited banter and how Matt looked at his daughter with such love. Once again, she forgave him for not letting Jade sing at the pageant. It was clear he was trying hard to protect her and keep her safe.

Warmth filled her heart. She was having a good time.

"Dad, can I be excused?" Jade spooned in her last bit of ice cream. "I want to show Ivy her new toys and see if she'll play with Holly."

"Oh, sure, go ahead."

They were alone at the table and now Serena felt nervous.

"Just curious. Who's the photographer of all your pictures?" she asked, trying to deflect from her jitters.

"I am."

Serena stood and moved closer to study the photos, then turned to face him. "You're very good. Your attention to detail is incredible."

Matt shrugged. "It's just something I enjoy. A good peaceful hobby."

"Well, you have a terrific eye."

"Thank you."

It amused her how his face turned red.

"You also did an amazing job with the party details. Jade seemed thrilled by all of it."

"Thanks again." He got up and started picking up the dishes.

"Did she not want the other students here?" Yes, she was being nosy, but she was also curious.

"No, she didn't. I'm surprised. I'm hoping it's not because she didn't want to bother me. She's done that in the past. It's my fault for being so busy while she was growing up, but I've tried hard to show her I've changed and she's my first priority."

"Well, sounds like the puppy was a fantastic idea that went over well."

He smiled. "Yes, she's a huge animal lover."

"Just like you."

"Like my wife, too."

Should she venture out and talk about her? See if he wanted to? After all, he was the one who brought it up.

"Maya sounds like quite a special person."

He turned his head and stared out the window for a few minutes.

"She was," he said softly. "I didn't deserve her."

Serena waited to see if he'd say more.

He didn't, but his eyes looked so sad as they turned back to hers, they almost brought her to tears.

I've got to get out of here.

"Well, I'd better go." She jumped up. She knew she was being abrupt, but she liked being around him way too much. Her affectionate feelings were exploding, as well as the instinct to reach out and comfort him. She fought the urge to hug him. She just couldn't allow herself to do that. She took a deep breath, trying to slow her racing heart. She needed to stay away. She had no time for this, and besides, there was no way he'd even be interested in her after being married to such a special person as Maya.

"So soon?" Jade entered the kitchen, both dogs following her.

"Yes, sorry. I have to help my mother bake." A lie, but it was either fib or get further sucked into caring for this little family.

She left in a hurry and all the way home thought of how sweet Matt was to his daughter. And to Holly. And how thoughtful he was to give Jade ballet lessons and a little pup to love.

He was also still incredibly sad over the loss of his wife.

This man was fast taking over her heart. Tugging at her feelings.

Totally against her will.

Seventeen

Serena woke the next day with a huge smile on her face. It was the day she would meet her students and their parents to build and paint the set for the pageant.

Dear God, she prayed. *Thank you so much for the gift of Jade, who showed us the way.*

Things had improved enormously since that special night at the bakery. Jade had managed to focus everyone in a way Serena couldn't. Her talk of love and the child Jesus and the secret giving to others in need had set the class abuzz. Everyone wanted to take part in Angel Heart Gifts and their eagerness spilled over to the pageant. All was going well. It was far from polished, but at least looked better, even without having found a singer. The group seemed to be filled with purpose, and she had renewed hope it would not be a fiasco on the night they performed. Glancing at her watch, she decided she'd better get up. She wanted to get there early to have everything set up and ready before the troops arrived.

Ouch.

Her arm hurt as she maneuvered out of bed.

While preparing for class the night before, she'd let another tray of buns burn and had to begin again. Her arm was still sore from all the stirring she'd done. Soon, she giggled, she'd have to start lifting weights to build up the muscle needed to get batches of goodies ready. She wondered how her mother and Helen did it. Years of experience, she guessed, having the timing down so they knew how many strokes were needed to produce the best batter. They also didn't burn anything. She still needed to get that right, for she wasted ingredients and they couldn't afford to do so. At least she scraped the burned parts off, freezing them and eating them herself. But she had to get better at that. She'd be disappointed if her attempt to help only turned into a hindrance. That was all her mother needed.

Now where was Holly? Used to be she'd be cuddling in bed with her in the morning. Not anymore.

Yawning, she slowly stood and worked her way over to the window. Glancing out, she watched the two dogs romping in the snow. Although Holly had been with Serena all night, she looked like she enjoyed her playtime with Gloria in the morning. Seemed she had developed the habit of sneaking out of bed and hanging by the door first thing, waiting for Mary to let her out. She used to do it once or twice a week, now it was every day. It was sweet how she had a furry best friend, but Serena missed her warm snuggles in the morning. Oh well, at least her pet was happy and that was all that mattered.

Now, get moving.

Showering and dressing quickly, she headed down to the bakery. Out of habit, she stopped to envelop herself in the many glorious smells, envisioning wearing them like warm, snuggly pajamas. She eventually pulled out of her trance and poured herself a coffee to go.

"Here you go, dear," her mother said, walking out of the kitchen with a box full of goodies. "A gift for you and your helpers." She also handed over a separate bag. "And breakfast for you, as well."

"A cinnamon roll?" Serena asked.

"You bet. Defrosted and iced." Her mom smiled. "Just the way you like it."

"One of my burnt ones, I hope?"

"Yes. Not too burned, though. You're too hard on yourself. More like, well done."

"Okay, Mom. But thanks for this."

"No problem, honey." Mary hurried back behind the counter and started placing cookies on a platter, getting ready for customers to arrive.

"I don't suppose you'd let me pay for them?" Serena asked.

"No thanks. I always supply food for the class when they build the set."

Another thing Serena didn't know, although now that her mom mentioned it, she did remember platters of cupcakes when she was a kid helping with the set. She also recalled her mother hammering and nailing late into the night as well.

Once again it hit her that her mother's kindness never ended.

"Thanks again, Mom."

"No problem. Just being supportive to our wonderful community. I hope the set gets finished today so you don't have to worry anymore."

"I'm counting on it. I also hope I don't devour all these baked goods on the way over in the car." She peeked in the bag. "Especially the brownies."

Her mother laughed. "Stick to your own bun, but you're welcome to the others, too. Come back and get more if you run out."

How did her mom get to be so amazing, thought Serena for about the one hundredth time, as she drove over to the church. She was always there for everyone. Too bad her own daughter couldn't be there for her at such a time of need. Her plan to save the bakery appeared to be failing.

Once again, a sense of urgency overtook her like a tenacious friend pushing her forward.

She had to make this pageant work. Things were improving, but she had to keep on trying. And she had to get that job. She just had to. Too much was at stake. She was determined to build the best set ever for this pageant and she so hoped she had a lot of skilled builders today. Hammering and sawing was not in her comfort zone.

Surprisingly, there were two trucks already in the parking lot when she arrived. Helpers or just there for the night? She wasn't sure.

She jumped out, opened the trunk, pulled out several bags and the treats, closed it and turned, almost running into someone right behind her.

"Oh, sorry," she said, looking up, way up.

Wait. She knew this person.

"Nick? Is that you again?"

"Yes," he smiled. "Me, again, minus the hat and glasses."

"Imagine running into you twice in a week."

"Well, this time isn't by accident. I popped into the bakery this morning and your mom said you were looking for help. Thought I'd come by and pitch in."

"Oh, okay. Thanks."

That was surprising. But she welcomed any help. Anything to get this done and over with.

"May I carry a few bags for you?"

"That'd be great. You'll save me an extra trip." She re-opened the trunk and pulled out a bigger box.

She handed it over to him, plus several bags.

"Got it all?" he asked.

"Yes. You're a big help."

Entering the foyer of the church, she heard voices. Who was in the hall already? It was early. She knew the minister had planned to leave the door open for her, but figured she'd be the first one there.

"I wonder who that is?" she asked.

"Early bird helpers. I saw them go in." Nick put down the box and bags, checking his pockets for something. "I'll be right back. Forgot my phone in the car and I can't live without it. You go ahead. I'll bring the stuff down when I come back."

"Thank you."

He took off while she continued down the stairs and stopped in her tracks. Jade and Matt stood there smiling at her. Nancy was beside them in full running attire, having obviously jogged over to join them.

She grinned at Nancy and Jade, but didn't know how to handle Matt. She was stunned to see him there.

What was he doing?

He hadn't signed up to help. Embarrassingly, she'd checked, hoping he'd be there, also at the same time hoping he wouldn't. She had noticed every student in the pageant had a father or mother arriving, except Jade.

"Hi, Ms. Davis. Dad came. Is that okay?" asked Jade, hurrying over to greet her.

"Of course it is. The more help the better."

The girl beamed. "I was so excited, we got here early and brought in the boxes in the hallway. They had your name on them, so we thought we'd help you out."

"Oh, thank you. That's the supplies we'll need. The caretaker of the school said he'd drop them off."

Serena was delighted to see how excited Jade was. Was it because her dad was here? She looked over at Matt.

"Thanks for helping."

"Yeah, great, huh?" Jade cut in. "I forgot to put his name down because I figured he'd be too busy to come."

"Never too busy to help you, honey." His eyes were tender as he glanced at his daughter, then back at Serena. "Jade said you needed parents as well to build the set. So, I'm here." He pointed to a tool kit sitting beside him. "I'm ready to do anything you need."

"Oh, great. But you didn't sign up, so I wasn't expecting you."

Get it together, Serena. She sounded rude, harping on something trivial. She'd even managed to shock Nancy, who had raised her eyebrows at her harsh words. Matt was here and ready to help, that was all that was important.

"But I'm glad you're able to join us," she added quickly, softening her tone.

"I was able to shift things around."

"Yes," Jade agreed. "He said I'm more important than his business deals."

She looked pleased, but Serena noted a quick flash of emotion surge through Matt's eyes.

"It's about time," he said. "So please, put me to work."

Interesting. Seemed like some tension going on there. Guilt, perhaps? Matt did mention at the party how he was once terribly busy. Sounded like he used to put work before his family. Was that why Jade looked so happy now? She was finally his priority? Looked like it was still a sore spot for Matt.

Stop it. She was jumping to conclusions. And where was Nancy when she needed her? Usually she'd jump in and smooth everything over. Looking around frantically, she finally noticed her friend off in the back, changing from her running shoes into work boots.

"Hello, Matt." Nick walked over to join them.

"Oh, right. Matt," Serena said, tilting her head towards Nick. "Do you remember this guy from school?"

Matt looked surprised and a bit annoyed, judging from the squeezed together eyebrows, not to mention his frown.

"Certainly." He reached out to shake his hand, reluctantly, it looked like. "Nick Aldred. Are you here to help?"

"Yes, I am," Nick said. "Didn't realize you were back in town."

"Didn't know you were still here."

"Well, I did leave for school, but came back when I graduated."

Serena sensed coolness between them, so quickly interjected, "Matt, Jade, I was wondering if you could start building the stable scene over there." She pointed to a space in the middle of the room. "I know this is what your daughter wanted to work on."

"Sure do." Jade grinned and once again her excitement overflowed. It was becoming infectious for Serena found herself responding back with a smile.

"Well, I'll show you where the materials are. Nick, I'll be right back to get you started on another project. Meanwhile, would you mind unpacking these boxes?"

"Sure, no problem."

She led Matt and Jade to where she wanted the creche scene built. "I had some lumber dropped off. It's over there up against the wall. Fortunately, we were lucky, a parent donated it all for free. Your daughter has a lot of plans for this."

"Yeah, Dad. I've been thinking of it for days," Jade said. She pulled a notebook out of her backpack. "I already showed this to Ms. Davis, and she approved it." She flipped through a few pages, found the one she wanted and held it out for her dad to see.

"Looks good and well-designed," he said, after studying it. "Well done. No problem at all. Go ahead and direct me, honey. You're in charge."

Jade got busy fast, opening the box and pulling out the tools she needed.

"I had no idea she was so creative," Matt said.

"She certainly is," agreed Serena. "And her enthusiasm is a blessing."

"Lately, especially. I'm relieved to see she seems much happier than she was." He paused, his face suddenly looking serious. "So... about Nick. Are you still good friends with him?"

"No. Not at all. Just ran into him the other day."

"Oh."

He looked like he was about to say something, but didn't.

"Do you remember Nancy?" asked Serena.

He smiled. "Of course I do. I also remember the two of you used to be inseparable."

"We lost touch for a while, but it's sure great reconnecting again."

"Hey, Dad, where are you?" shouted Jade, on the other side of the lumber pile. "I need you."

"Well, I'd better get to work."

"Thanks for helping. I appreciate it," Serena said.

She watched them for a while, marveling at how happy Jade was to be working with her father. Seemed like they were developing a strong bond, which was lovely to witness.

Hearing a group of people chatting as they walked in the door, she hurried over to greet them. In approximately twenty minutes, all the students had showed up and most of their parents, including a few uncles, aunts and friends sprinkled in as well. It was going to be a good day...she was sure of it.

Serena quickly got to work showing them what was needed—the inn, the decorations, props. She added Nick to the inn group, based on his knowledge of construction. She then asked a few students and their helpers to build the special donation boxes, overseen by Nancy. They would be passed around on the pageant night, as well as be located by the door as per tradition. She needed to remind herself to discuss with the students where this year's donation would go. She was curious as to what their main cause would be. She did hear them mention a lunch program at the church to serve those in need, which would be wonderful. She grinned again, acknowledging how happy her heart was. Her students all seemed to be working as a team for a change, busy directing their entourage, which was more than she had dreamed of. Even Jacob was busy helping with the inn, accompanied by his dad, Julie, and her parents. She was thrilled at all the creating that was going on.

"You didn't tell me how good-looking Matt is."

"What?" Serena turned to find a grinning Nancy standing there. "He's not."

"Yes, he is. He was a cute kid, from what I recall, and I've seen a few photos here and there, but in person, he's downright handsome now. So are you sure there aren't any sparks flying?"

"None. How about with you and Nick?"

"Nick? I told you we don't keep in touch."

"Well, he's here."

"He is?"

She looked around. "I don't see him."

"He's over there." Serena pointed to the other side of the hall. "The guy with the baseball cap on."

"Oh." Nancy paused a moment to stare. "Nope, no sparks."

Serena laughed.

"You haven't talked to him yet."

"Well, it's all history now. I have no great need to talk with him or even reconnect, but I might go say hello. Just don't fool yourself. I saw a spark or two hovering around you and Matt earlier."

"No, you didn't. Now go on, get back to work."

She could hear Nancy laughing all the way back to her group of workers.

Serena wondered what her friend would think if she knew how much she did notice and think about Matt. All the time.

She glanced over at Jade and Matt. They were both hammering away, as well as chatting and laughing. She watched how animated his face was and felt drawn to go join them.

Stop.

Forget about him. He is an unnecessary distraction.

She turned her attention to Nick, who had connected with several students and was hard at work as well.

Watching him chat away, she was reminded of how these two men, Nick and Matt, certainly brought back memories. Some not so good.

Enough of that.

She didn't want to be reminded of old stuff, especially not right now. She turned away to watch several students build the step needed to elevate the angel when she stood behind the Holy Family. It was looking good.

"You look worried."

Serena jumped and turned to find Matt there. She hadn't seen him approach.

"Oh, guess I am. Just want everything to go well."

"It's more than that." His eyes filled with compassion. "You're concerned about your mother too, aren't you? And the bakery?"

She was surprised he was so perceptive.

"Well, yes."

"I'm sorry to hear it might be closing."

"Me, too. I keep hoping it won't." His concern touched her.

"Is there a possibility it can stay open?"

"Well, if I get hired full-time and have the money to pay for the building, we can keep Petals going."

"I hope it all works out for you. Do you stand a good chance to get the permanent teaching job?"

"Well..." She grinned. "If the pageant goes well."

"Oh. Well, sorry again about Jade not singing."

"Don't worry. I understand." And she did. The love he had for his daughter was obvious and she knew he was just protecting her.

"Well, I'd better get back to work. Jade is a hard taskmaster." He nodded towards his daughter, who was trying to carry a long piece of wood by herself. He ran over to help her.

After he left, Serena pulled out her laptop and got busy working on the program for the event. If she could finish this today, she'd not only have the set built but all paperwork finished as well.

"Excuse me."

She looked up to find Nick smiling at her.

"I'm sorry, but I have to leave." He tapped his phone. "A problem with a site I'm working on. I'd like to put it off and take care of it later, but my brother says it's urgent. Family business, you know."

"No problem." She reached out to shake his hand. "Thanks for your help."

"And don't worry. The props are done, and the inn is pretty much finished. They're just painting a final coat on it." He pointed over to the group of students diligently working their brushes over the wood.

"Thanks. I see that. And you did a good job. It's kind of you to help out in the first place."

"Well, after all, I owe you." His eyes flicked to the ceiling, as if he were finding it hard to look at her.

That was odd.

"You do? For what?"

"Never thought you'd talk to me again after I threw that banana peel on the stage the day of our own pageant." He jerked his head down to look directly at her. "I'm sorry about that. It was a dumb move. Couldn't figure out why you forgave me so fast, but I always considered myself lucky."

Her heart thudded.

So, it was true? Matt was right? Someone had tried to sabotage her dancing? And it was Nick? Her friend at the time?

"You're kidding. You did that?" She knew her voice sounded harsh, but she just couldn't help it.

He looked puzzled. "I thought you knew."

"No, of course I didn't." She stepped back, wanting distance between them. "You said Matt threw it there."

"And you believed me? I denied it, but figured Matt told you the truth. After all, he saw me toss it."

"I thought he made that up and I believed you. After all, I'd known you longer. We were good friends. I didn't know Matt as well."

"Sorry." He glanced over at Matt. "But he told the truth."

"Why would you do something like that?"

He shook his head. "I was a silly kid and jealous as anything."

"Jealous? Why?"

"You seemed to like Matt and I had a huge crush on you."

Serena's mouth fell open. "You did? So you thought you'd make me fall?"

"Well, I never said I was bright. I was nearby, watching you closely and figured you'd slip and I'd rush out and save you. I'd be the hero and I'd blame it all on Matt. After all, he was the so-called stage director at the time. And then you'd like me more."

Her head spun.

To think she hadn't believed Matt, and even stopped talking to him way back then.

Amazing how the past creeped up at times with the acknowledgment that old hurts can last a lifetime. And some of them could be based on falsehoods.

"I don't know what to say."

"It was a rotten thing for me to do. I thought it was a safe prank, but I later realized you could have gotten hurt."

Yes, it was rotten, and she could have easily gotten injured.

"Well, guess we were just kids." She said this fast, not wanting to deal with it now.

"No excuse. May I take you out for dinner sometime. To cement my apology?"

No.

But maybe she had to learn to forgive and leave it all in the past. Just not now. It was still too raw and had cost her a friendship with Matt.

"I'll think about it."

"Fair enough. I'll call you." He glanced at his watch. "Gotta go."

She noticed he turned and waved to Nancy before walking out the door. She also saw that Nancy waved back. Guess they'd made contact after all. She'd have to talk to her about that later, but first, she had to clear something up. Right now. It had gone on too long.

She hurried over to Matt.

"May I speak to you for a second?"

"Okay."

"Privately?"

She led him off to the side where they could talk alone.

"Am I in trouble?" he asked.

He looked nervous, just like he had that day at Petals. Like a little boy caught in a bad act of some kind.

"Not at all. I owe you a huge apology."

"You do?" He looked shocked. His eyebrows reached upwards and he took a step back.

"Yes, remember I was so mad at you for closing the curtain when I danced at our pageant?"

"Yes, I will never forget that."

"Well, Nick just confirmed your story about the banana peel. I'm so sorry I ever doubted you."

His eyes lit up and he looked delighted.

"So, he owned up to it after all this time?"

"Yes, he did."

"Well, my respect for him has grown immensely. I'm just glad we got it all cleared up. Years later, but still a good thing."

"The truth is, you in fact saved me by closing that curtain and grabbing the banana peel. I could have been seriously injured."

"That's why I did it."

She shook her head. "And to think I didn't believe you."

"That's okay. You know the truth now."

"Dad, I need you," a loud voice shouted out.

"That's Jade. I have to go. We're just about to lift up the framework."

"No problem. I'll come too."

She followed him over, noting they were raising the structure for the manger scene. She joined in and slowly they put it up, carefully resting it on two leg guards attached from the other side.

"Brilliant work," Serena said, clapping her hands. "Well done."

She stepped back to get a better view.

Oh, no.

Tripping over a piece of wood, she went down fast. Preparing herself for huge pain, her arms flew out…

Moving at lightning speed, Matt grabbed her, wrapping his arms around her waist. She looked up into worried eyes.

"Are you okay?" he whispered.

"Yes."

But not really. At least from an emotional point of view.

Her heart pounded. Her cheeks flushed.

"Thanks for saving me," she said, liking his touch way too much. "For the second time."

Were Matt's cheeks flushed, too?

Was his face lowering to hers?

"Where are you, Dad?" shouted Jade. "We're going to add more wood to make it a lot securer. We need your help."

Whew. Saved.

Eighteen

Reluctantly, Matt let go of Serena. Slowly, carefully.

"Are you okay? Are you hurt?" he asked, backing away.

"No, I'm fine."

"Good. Well, I have to get back to work."

"Me, too."

He hurried over to help Jade and her friends secure the prop. He knew he'd been abrupt, but had to get away.

"Looks good, right, Dad?" Jade asked.

"It's perfect. You did an amazing job of designing and building it."

"Thanks. But everyone helped. Great team effort."

He noticed Jade was literally shining, basking in his praise, and a stab of sadness sliced through him. He had missed so many of these moments when she was small, too busy making deals and stuck in his office. He had to continue working to change that. He had to try harder. The joy in Jade's eyes was all he needed to motivate him. Shaking his head in frustration, he wondered how he had never noticed this and how his priorities had been all mixed up. Money over family was so wrong. He should have known better.

Since the nativity scene seemed pretty much finished, he walked over to the refreshment table and grabbed a water. He needed to cool down.

Having Serena in his arms had startled him.

His face had even flushed, as he cursed the fact that he reddened at times when embarrassed or caught unawares, something he'd been dealing with all his life. What was worse was he wanted to keep on holding her. In that brief moment, he was reminded of two things: how much he had liked her as a kid and how wonderful the power of touch was. Instinctively, relieved, moved by the fact she wasn't hurt, he had almost kissed her.

Right in the middle of a work session with his daughter standing there.

Was he insane?

Had to admit though, he missed the comfort of affection from a woman, the exhilaration, and most of all, the love.

Love?

Why was he thinking about love?

He didn't love Serena.

He had loved his wife.

Hadn't he?

To be honest, at times he wondered.

Maya had been a wonderful person, but sometimes he questioned if he had been so much in love with her, why was it so hard to curtail his work life? Wouldn't he have wanted to be home with her? Wouldn't he at least have listened to her? And tried harder to make things work?

Questions haunted him daily.

He couldn't find peace. He couldn't find closure.

He caught sight of a painting of Jesus hanging on the wall near the stage. He stared, mesmerized, a moment of reckoning. He didn't deserve love, or to find anyone special again. He had let down his wife and his daughter. He needed to pay for that.

Guilt hit. Again.

It was his constant companion these days, an old familiar friend. No, not a friend, but a foe. As well as letting everyone else down, he had let Serena down too. Seemed to be how he lived his life these days. Never measuring up. He was at least happy she'd found out the truth from Nick. He had only been protecting her all those years ago. Saving her from a fall, and he was glad she knew that. Now he didn't appear so much of an ogre as in the past. He could still recall how hurt he had been when she started ignoring him after the pageant.

Hearing Serena's laughter, he watched the ease with which she chatted amid a group of students. He could understand now why it meant so much to her to have Jade sing. Why she was desperate. He could see the pain in her eyes when she talked about losing the bakery. She had a lot at stake and here he refused to get involved. Basically, refusing to save Petals.

He contemplated leaving the room fast.

Just running out the door and immersing himself in work to forget his muddled thoughts, but couldn't do that to his daughter. Besides, this set needed more work.

"Dad, I need you again." This time Jade sounded impatient.

He realized he was just standing there, alternating between staring at the picture and Serena. Here he was trying to help Jade, to make up for past slights, and he was doing it again. Off track, as always. She was probably tired of having to call him over.

"Coming."

He hurried over to his daughter.

"What's up?" he asked.

"Could you please hold these boards while I hammer?" She still sounded frustrated. He didn't blame her.

"Sure can." Glad of the diversion from his other thoughts, he was at least proud he'd taught Jade how to use tools. Surprisingly, she was just as good at hammering as he was, taught to him by his own dad. She had been working with Jacob on a cradle to place the baby Jesus in and doing a good job.

"Oh, and did you tell Ms. Davis about the straw?" she asked.

"Straw?" Jacob said. "Cool."

"Not yet." Matt smiled. "I figured I'd give you the honors."

"Thanks."

She hammered away, finished, then took off. Matt saw her talking to Serena. In a few seconds she was back.

"Yep, she wants the straw."

"Okay, I'll bring it in." He headed to the door, glad to get out of that room for some air. The greater the space between him and Serena, the better.

"Dad, wait."

He stopped and looked back to find Jade running after him.

"It's heavy," she said. "I'll gather some of my friends to help carry it."

It was nice to hear she had friends and judging by her many greetings back and forth today, she felt more comfortable at Angel. At least something was working out.

A group of students accompanied him to the car and as they carefully carried the bales back to the church, he could hear Jade singing away. A sign she was happy.

Once again, he registered that her voice was astonishing. It had matured with age and for the first time he could hear what Maya heard—that it was richer than hers. Better even, although Maya's voice was incredible.

Doubt set in.

Should he let her sing "O Holy Night?" Especially since it could save the bakery?

No way. Don't think like that.

He couldn't take the chance. No, his mind was made up...he wasn't letting her.

After they brought in the hay, Jade leaned over and whispered, "Dad, can I sing at the pageant? I really want to, and we need a singer. Please?"

He stared at her pleading face. It was as if she sensed his struggle and was weighing in on what she wanted. Maybe he was in the wrong.

"I'll think about it."

"Okay. That's at least better than a no."

"The stable looks amazing," Serena said, coming over. "The straw is the extra special touch. Thank you for thinking of it. Well done."

He could barely look at her.

"Yeah, it does look pretty good," said an excited Jade.

"It does and hey, there are baked goods over there, just waiting for you to eat them. Help yourself."

While Jade and the rest of the students ate, joined by Serena, parents and all the helpers, Matt walked away fast and put his tools in the car.

Arriving back, he glanced at the door with the word chapel on it. Jade had shown him the room the other day.

Surprisingly, he felt drawn to drop in.

Should he?

Making a quick decision, he opened the door and hurried in, walked straight to the front, knelt and looked around. Candles glowed and, with the dim lighting, it appeared ethereal, heavenly, calming, soothing. Inspired by this, all sorts of peaceful feelings arose amid his torment.

He looked up at another picture of Jesus...this time He was gently holding a lamb. The compassion in His eyes slowly thawed Matt's heart.

He decided to pray, probably for the first time in years.

"God," he said softly. "I know I don't deserve to be here, nor do I deserve to ask You to listen to me. I have basically abandoned You these past two years."

He hung his head. Thoughts of Jade and Maya walked across his mind, as if parading on a stage.

"I crave direction now. I worry about so many things and I don't know what I'm supposed to do anymore."

He raised his eyes to a candle, watching it flicker and dance. How sad that his own light had been completely extinguished. It was gone.

And he was still angry.

Angry that his world had changed.

Angry that his wife had died.

Angry that he never knew what the right thing was for Jade.

Serena's mother joined his crowded thoughts. Along with Serena's worry stricken face.

"Should I, God? Should I let Jade sing? The Petals' bakery is in jeopardy and my daughter's singing might be able to help. But I am afraid of what it might lead to. I'm afraid of losing her."

His heart wrenched as he recalled the days of sitting by Maya's bedside, hoping and praying she'd come out of her coma. When he finally realized his wife was not coming back, he had promised her he'd be a better person and take good care of their daughter. It was a vow he had bombed. Jade did seem happier here in Angel, but she was not able to do the things she loved. Music being one of them. He had basically shut her down.

Closing his eyes, he allowed the silence of the chapel to envelop him and still his mind. Taking long breaths in and out, a sense of peace finally infiltrated him.

Slowly, an answer formed.

There was only one clear response.

The right one.

He jumped up and headed back to the hallway.

He knew exactly what he had to do.

Finally.

Nineteen

"Sure you don't want me to stay longer?" asked Nancy, looking around the room.

"No, no. We're done." Serena breathed a huge sigh of relief. "Lots of work, but the set looks good."

"More than good. It's the best I've ever seen."

"Well, it was all because of my helpers, so thank you for joining us."

"Oh, it was fun. Your students were excited and enthusiastic, and I enjoyed helping them." Nancy sat, pulling off her boots, changing back into her running shoes.

"They are pretty great. But hey, you still haven't told me how it felt to reconnect with Nick?"

"Oh, it was nothing." She stood, pulling on her coat.

Was she blushing? thought Serena.

"So, in all these years, you never ran into him. Shocking."

"Well, I was away at school, so was he. He's only been back about a year, and guess our paths just never crossed. Anyway, now that you've told me about how he was the one responsible for that whole banana peel fiasco, he's not so appealing anymore."

"It was definitely a childish trick. Seems like he at least feels remorse, so that's something. Guess we've all done things we're not proud of."

"Maybe." Nancy picked up her knapsack. "Are you sure you don't want me to sweep the floor one last time?"

It was obvious she didn't want to talk about Nick. Just like Serena didn't want to talk about Matt.

Did he almost kiss her? Should she get Nancy's take on it?

No, don't think about that.

It was too complicated.

"Oh, it's fine," she quickly answered Nancy. "You go on home before it gets dark. After all, you're jogging, I'm driving. Why you won't let me take you, I'll never know."

"I'm fine. Running is my happy place. So, I'll see you later. Take care."

"Bye. Thanks again for helping."

Serena waved her away, then walked over to turn the lights off. She looked around one last time.

The set really did look amazing.

Freshly painted, everything in its place, straw making it appear authentic, it fit the class's vision exactly. She even smiled at the inn—a large wooden structure securely propped up and tied with thick rope. The innkeeper and his wife would make an appearance through a cut-out hole the size of a window. It'd been painted a brilliant blue with white trim and sketched across it were luxurious window boxes holding colored flowers. The students had decided to have it look rich and lavish to contrast with the browns and blacks that represented the poorer stable scene. It might not be exactly historical or accurate, but certainly proved their point of making their pageant effective with huge messages to share.

Excitement and anticipation raced through her.

She sure hoped it all turned out well on pageant night. At least she felt more optimistic than she had in ages.

"Well done."

Serena jumped, not aware anyone else was around.

"Sorry to startle you," the principal said. "Just thought I'd take a peek. I heard you had a good turnout to help build this."

Amazing that this man had arrived twice now without Serena ever hearing him. Was it on purpose to catch her unawares? Possibly doing something wrong? Or coincidence? She decided it must be a fluke. He couldn't possibly be checking up on her, could he?

"Er, yes we did." She sounded like a schoolgirl.

Snap out of it.

"Every student was here, sir," she continued. "As well as at least one parent, if not both, and several friends and relatives."

"Well, it looks wonderful and I admire its originality and creativity. The straw adds a nice touch and makes the whole stable scene seem exceptionally real. Good. I planned on helping as well, but had to take my grandchild to a hockey game." He shook his head. "Both my son and daughter-in-law were overbooked. We all get so busy at times."

"We do, sir."

"So, you're all ready?"

Well, no singer, but she wasn't going to tell him that yet, if ever. He'd find out soon enough.

"I am." She tried to sound confident.

"And I heard your classes are going well."

"Thank you. It's kind of you to let me know."

She wondered who told him all that. At least it was a good report.

"I understand you have also applied for the available job in the new year."

"Yes, sir. I most certainly have. I love this school and how you run it."

Was she gushing? She hoped not. While he might not be the warmest character around, his school was wonderful, and staff seemed happy, which of course trickled down to students. She meant what she said.

"Well, we are interviewing soon. I'll let you know."

Was that a twinkle in his eye? Was he smiling? Was that a good thing? Something positive? A clue she might be in the running?

"Thank you."

They walked out to the parking lot together and she waved goodbye as she got in her car. Judging by how supportive he was, it sounded as if he might be leaning towards her for the job. Once again, she figured the final decision may have a lot to do with how the pageant turned out. With no singer, it could be touch and go. She could only pray, cross her fingers and hope.

Now to get focused again.

First, she had to stop by Petals to pick up treats, then she was off to give Jade her first ballet lesson. Earlier, she had regretted having it on the evening of their set building. She figured they'd be tired, but the wonderful day left her feeling she could run a marathon if needed. It should be fun, considering this girl was a pleasure to be around. She looked forward to it.

Happy, she turned up the radio and blared it, singing along to Christmas music. One of her favorites came on, so she sang even louder.

Joy to the world...

Lately, she sang every time she got in her car, hoping the delightful carols would keep her in good spirits. As Christmas drew nearer, she longed to be lifted from the sadness of possibly losing the bakery. Sometimes it worked. Often it didn't. Today it did. The set was built, the principal seemed to like her and maybe the whole pageant might not be a total loss. Hopefully, not.

The Lord has come...

Continuing to sing her loud rendition of "Joy to the World," she came to a stop outside the bakery. Every time she saw the for-sale sign, it felt like a knife sliced right through her heart.

She couldn't let that happen. She sang even louder as she walked down the walkway to the Petals, continuing to cheer herself up. This time *a cappella* without the accompaniment of the radio.

Let earth receive her king...

She opened the door.

"Hey," Mary shouted out. "Was that you singing out there?"

"Am I that loud?"

Her mother grinned.

"A little, but it was joy to my ears. Getting in the Christmas mood, I see. I wondered if there were carolers out there, so I ran to the window."

"Yeah, right, Mom." Serena laughed. "Bet you were wondering who was out there bellowing out of tune for all the world to hear. Hope I didn't scare any customers away."

"No, don't worry about that." Her mother pulled her into a hug. "I'm just surprised to see you. I thought you were teaching tonight."

"I am." No one hugged like her mother. Serena wrapped her own arms around her, loving the comfort it gave her.

"Are you not too tired?"

"No, the day went well, which energized me." Serena pulled back. "Just thought I'd grab a few snacks as a treat. Figured Jade would like that."

"Oh, it's Jade. What a great idea." Mary hurried behind the counter. "I'll put some hot chocolate in a thermos, and you can have it after with your treats. By the way, I also heard the set-building went well. Several students popped in and were gushing about it."

"Thanks, Mom. I'm pleased by how it all turned out. But here, let me help you. Jade should be there soon."

She gathered up some goodies along with the chocolate, kissed her mom goodbye and headed to the studio. Hurrying inside, she put the treats down in a small kitchen nook, quickly changed into tights and a t-shirt and began stretching at the barre in preparation. She'd lucked out when the local dance studio allowed her to use the space once a week.

"Your mother gives us free snacks during recital time, the least I can do is allow you to use the studio on nights when we don't need it," Janice Staples, the owner, had said.

What was amazing was that she refused rent.

"Mary won't take any money for her food, so no way will I take rent."

The money she made for the lessons went straight into her 'save the bakery' fund.

Twirling around the room, she allowed her body to be free and move to the music. Her days were filled to the brim, what with teaching and baking, and today, set building. Ballet lessons gave her a chance to work some good healthy exercise into her life. Dance was something she loved, and at one point was her whole life, until she decided education was the career field for her. She was still amazed she was completing her doctorate, once contemplating getting into administrative work with schools, but now discovering she truly loved teaching. As the days rolled on, she still found it fulfilling and utterly fascinating. It captivated her. She smiled remembering how excited Sally Watkins had been, when she received her first A in History.

"I studied hard, Ms. Davis. But I can't believe I did so well," she had said, with a proud look on her face.

Serena had answered back, *"You deserve every bit of it."* And Sally's smile grew larger.

And then Noah James had discovered he could speak with confidence in front of the class, when he had been avoiding doing that all through school. And Maria finally figured out her mathematic equations after crying in class, exclaiming she didn't understand the latest lesson. There were a lot of struggles and huge joys, and Serena got to witness it all. She especially loved the challenge of helping them in creative, individualistic ways.

"Hi there."

Serena skidded to a stop and looked over. She'd been so engrossed in her exercises and thoughts, she hadn't even heard the door open and shut. Maybe that was how Principal Lemire arrived—right in the middle of her daydreams where she somehow managed to block everything else out. Maybe he wasn't sneaking around at all.

"Oh, hi, Jade. Are you ready for your lesson?"

"Sure am." The young girl pulled off her coat to reveal a bright pink leotard over pale blue tights. With her blonde hair tied back into a chignon, she was the vision of a professional ballet dancer.

"You look amazing."

"Um, thanks. I picked this up with my mother a few years ago. Fortunately, I still fit into it. I love the color pink."

"It also suits you. You are literally glowing."

"Awww...thanks."

Serena looked behind her.

"Is your dad here?"

"No. He dropped me off and left."

Good. He was mostly a distraction but at the same time, she felt disappointed. She was getting in the habit of enjoying his visits, comments and little jolts of humor. Almost looking forward to them.

"But guess what?" Jade said. "I have some exciting news."

"What?" The girl's eyes were wide and she looked like she could barely contain her excitement.

"I can't wait to tell you." She jumped up and down and performed a little pirouette. "I need to cue a drumbeat. Dad said I can sing 'Holy Night.'"

Serena, who had been moving nearer to hear the news, stopped in her tracks. Had she heard right?

"Pardon? Did you say you are allowed to sing?"

"Yes. I can sing at the pageant."

Tears stung Serena's eyes. She closed her eyes for a moment.

Oh, dear God. Is this true?

Finally, she opened her eyes and said, "Oh, Jade. I am so honored that you can do this."

She tried to calm down, not wanting to get too excited because she was afraid of scaring Jade and putting even more pressure on her.

"I'm over the moon, Ms. Davis. I just want to help, and using a tape is silly when I know the whole song."

"Thank you. You have such a good heart and we can practice anytime you like."

"Great. I need to. I'm nervous and I might have to get used to using a microphone again."

"No problem. And your dad is okay with this?"

She still couldn't believe it.

"Yes. It was his idea."

"Amazing."

Jade threw herself into Serena's arms.

"I'm so happy."

"Me, too," Serena whispered, surprised by her warm hug.

The girl pulled back. "Well..." She grinned. "Guess I'm ready for my lesson now."

"Have you taken much ballet before?"

"A little and it was when I was a lot younger. And I'm not very good. Then I got involved in singing and riding horses, and after my mom died, I dropped dance class completely. Along with singing, but that was mainly because of my dad."

"Well, let's begin with basic stretches. I have some Christmas music I thought I'd put on to get us in the mood. Will that be okay?"

"Love it."

"Now, let's warm up."

Jade sang along as she stretched and moved and danced. Along with a beautiful voice, she had such grace as well, so much so that Serena was impressed. This girl was loaded with talent, she thought, as she ran her through more exercises and at the end said, "Okay. Now let's dance from the heart."

"Pardon?"

"Just let loose. It's very freeing. Just go and do what your body wants to do. Move any way you want."

"Will you do that with me?"

"I'd be honored."

And they both began to dance.

Completely, from the heart.

Twenty

Matt glanced up from the legal document he was reviewing to check his watch. Time to pick up his daughter, a nice respite from paperwork for his growing clientele in Angel.

He'd been lucky. He'd never expected to have so much business so fast, but the key lawyer in town had retired the previous year, so he was pretty much it around here. Previously, folks had to travel to nearby towns to seek counsel and seemed thrilled that another lawyer had moved to Angel. He had almost more work than he could handle.

Standing, stretching, he walked over to see how Ivy was doing. She'd already eaten, played with a stuffed rabbit, run around the yard and had passed out on her bed. Her eyes were open now, watching him, and he noticed she also glanced at his hands. It'd taken her no time at all to realize that humans sometimes carried treats.

"Hey, Ivy, want to come with me to fetch Jade?"

He smiled as the little dog's tail began wagging.

"I take it that's a yes," he said, as he bent down to snap a leash on her. It was bright pink, Jade's favorite color, which matched the dog's pink faux-jewelled collar. The other day in the barn, James teased him about how unmanly it looked, but if it made his daughter happy, it was all he cared about.

Throwing on his coat, he led the pup out to the yard for a potty break, then settled her in the truck and took off towards town. Every house he passed had Christmas lights shouting good cheer. Maybe he should take a stab at decorating his own place. Jade would love it and it could be a real bonding experience. Even though he didn't feel in the Christmas spirit, maybe trying would get him in the mood.

Realizing he was early, he stopped at Petals. Might as well get some goodies; Jade would be delighted.

Pulling to a stop, he grimaced at the for-sale sign. Once again, he felt it was a tragedy that this bakery would eventually be closed down. He still wondered if he could help in any way.

Walking in the door, holding Ivy in his arms, he could immediately smell fresh bread baking. And cinnamon buns. His stomach rumbled in anticipation, as Serena's mother came through the door.

"It's Matt Jenkins, right?"

He smiled. "Yes. And you are Mrs. Davis?"

"I am. I remember you as a little boy coming in here for cookies. Chocolate chip, right?"

"Good memory. And I still love them. They're the best I've ever had anywhere."

"Well, thank you. And who do you have here?"

"Ivy, my daughter's pup. I hope you don't mind that I carried her in. I'm only going to be a few minutes and I don't trust her not to get into trouble if I leave her alone in the truck."

"Not at all." She leaned over to pat Ivy's head. "I'm a huge dog lover myself. In fact, I have one named Gloria."

"Good to know."

"So, how may I help you?"

"Well, I'm picking up Jade and I'd like a couple of cookies and two cinnamon buns, along with two hot chocolates to go."

"Well, you can have that, of course, but I believe my daughter is with yours at the moment and Serena was already here collecting treats."

He laughed.

"Oh, okay. Then how about a hot chocolate and cookie for me? To go. Oh, and a cinnamon bun."

"Coming right up."

She poured the hot drink, placed several cookies in a bag, along with a cinnamon bun, and set it all on a takeout tray.

"How much?" he asked.

"On the house."

"No way."

"Yes, I insist."

She handed him the tray which he found easy to carry—food in one hand, dog in the other.

He couldn't keep his eyes off this thoughtful woman.

Should he? Why not.

"Mrs. Davis."

"Oh, please call me Mary."

"Well…Mary. If you ever need a lawyer for anything, please don't hesitate to call me. On the house, of course."

She looked surprised.

"Well, thank you. I just might need some legal advice soon. I'll pay, of course."

"You already have." He waved the tray. "Just give me a call. I'll do anything to assist you." He put the drink and goodies down, dug out his card and handed it to her.

"Here's my number."

"Why, thank you."

Gathering up his loot again, he left, got back in his car and arrived at the studio a few blocks down. He sat there waiting, sipping the hot chocolate, not wanting to go in. He'd been avoiding Serena, embarrassed by her effect on him. The seconds ticked by fast and after ten minutes there was still no sign of his daughter. He'd have to go in after all, for she was likely waiting inside for him.

"C'mon, Ivy. Let's go."

He let her sniff around the front yard for a few minutes, then walked into the building and climbed the stairs to the dance studio. Jade had shown him where it was the other day. Christmas music blared and he looked through a glass window to see the two of them dancing, lost in their own worlds, moving to the music. To him, they resembled angels, dressed in white and pink, and he noticed occasionally they'd smile at each other, sharing their moment of joy. Then "O Holy Night" came on and Jade stopped, closed her eyes and sang along. Serena came to a halt as well, watching Jade, mesmerized.

Matt's heart exploded at the sound of his daughter's voice. Every time he heard it, he was touched. It was truly a blessing to be able to share this special moment, and he was glad he had given the okay for her to sing. Serena was right. It was a shame to keep that beauty hidden. She needed to shine for the glory of God and he was glad he had finally figured it out that day in the chapel.

Serena clapped.

Full of accolades, he was about to walk in the door when he heard Jade say, "I miss God, you know."

"You do?"

"Yes."

"Do you still pray?"

"Yes, but I miss going to church with Dad. We used to go all the time."

"Have you told him?"

"No, he won't listen."

His heart broke. Seemed he'd been so involved with his own issues of fear, he'd forgotten about his daughter's wishes. He had just reminded her again the other day to talk to him whenever she wanted. It was clear she couldn't. She'd kept the whole heart gifts project a secret and now how much she missed going to church with him. He had been a horrible husband and a bad father. Close-minded, set in his ways, and not listening to his daughter.

He knocked, then walked into the room, feeling he was eavesdropping and not wanting to hear any more confessions.

"Dad!" Jade looked startled. "And Ivy."

He glanced at Serena. "Hope you don't mind the pup here?"

"No, not at all. Feel free to let her down."

He handed Ivy over to Jade, who quickly hugged her, then put her on the floor to explore her surroundings. She giggled at the little pup climbing on her backpack by the door, sniffing away.

"She probably smells my apple," Jade said.

"Go ahead and give her some water, if you want," Serena said. "There's a little kitchenette over there." She pointed to the left part of the room. "Plus hot chocolate and treats for you."

"Well, thanks." Jade's eyes lit up. "Come here, Ivy. Follow me."

She led her to the room and Matt could hear her say, "There you go, little one. Something to drink."

Matt smiled at how loving his daughter was to Ivy. A true animal lover.

Serena walked over. "Thank you so much for allowing Jade to sing."

She looked so happy; Matt had to look away fast so as not to be caught staring.

"It's the right thing to do."

To his surprise, Serena leaned over and hugged him.

Instinctively he put his arms around her and when she pulled back, he couldn't help but stare at her lips.

Again.

If Jade weren't there, he had no idea what he'd do. Once again it seemed instinctual, natural.

A sinking feeling hit him

Stop it.

He was in trouble. Big, big trouble. He liked Serena way too much, and it was definitely too soon. It was just she was so familiar to him, like an old friend he'd reconnected with who was safe and caring, yet exciting and fun. Not to forget compassionate and kind.

No, he couldn't do this.

He had no idea how she'd even react. Or his daughter.

He pushed away fast. "C'mon Jade," he yelled. "Gather up Ivy and let's go."

Serena looked startled and he knew he sounded rude.

Just couldn't help it.

Fear was a powerful thing and he needed to get away.

Fast.

Twenty-one

Matt was up bright and early and off to the barn.

As a matter of fact, he had barely slept, troubled by his constant worry about Jade, and his unease about how Serena continued to creep into his thoughts. Nonstop. He felt increasingly drawn to her and he had to stop that. He didn't need anything to interfere in his main goal, which was to protect Jade.

So glad I have lots of chores to do, he thought, as he began feeding the horses and mucking out stalls. Keeping busy helped him at least try to keep his mind off stuff, even though he was doing the very thing he had hired people to do. They gave him quizzical looks here and there as he whirl-winded through the barn, but he needed this. Gave him something physical to immerse himself in, rather than just think thoughts that were never resolved.

Next, he settled down in his office, face-timed a client away on vacation, set up appointments, and wrote a few letters. It struck him that he would soon have to hire a secretary to keep up with his busy law firm. Work piled high and he needed help to get through it all in a timely fashion.

He glanced at his watch.

Breakfast time.

Shutting down his computer, he headed to the kitchen.

Pancakes it was.

Jade would be down shortly, so he quickly got to work heating up the grill and blending together ingredients.

"Hi, Dad," she said, practically dancing down the stairs in riding clothes, her usual Sunday morning attire. Ivy trotted right behind her, yipping and yapping in her high-pitched puppy voice.

"Going riding, of course?"

"Sure am. Yummmm...pancakes."

"Your favorite. And I didn't skimp on the chocolate chips this time."

"Well, that's good. Thanks, Dad."

He placed the pile of pancakes on the table while she filled Ivy's bowls with food and water.

"Dig in," he said.

And she did, stacking at least three of them on top of each other, buttering them, pouring a river of syrup over the whole pile.

"Hey, save me some," he said, joining her at the table.

"I did." She giggled.

They ate in silence for a while, watching and laughing over Ivy's antics. The little pup had devoured her food almost in one gulp and was tossing a small stuffed frog around, enthralled by the toy's squeak.

"You're really enjoying her," Matt observed.

"Yes. Best buddy ever. Such a great birthday gift."

"You deserve her. Besides, she is very sweet. Growing bigger by the minute." Should he ask? Oh, why not. "Hey, how's the pageant coming along?" Once again, avoiding Serena on purpose, he'd missed a few practices. Couldn't help fishing for information though; he was curious.

"Getting better. I love that I can sing again. It's so much fun. Thanks again for letting me."

"No problem. I should never have enforced that rule."

"I know you were just looking out for me." She grinned. "But I'll be okay."

"I know you will." He didn't, but hoped. It was also nice seeing her smile more. "I'll always be worried, but I shouldn't stop you from doing what you love."

"And I love dancing and singing but..."

She sighed. Loudly.

"What's wrong? Are the pancakes no good? I notice you're slowing down."

"No way. They're perfect. Just wished the bakery wasn't going to close. I love that place and sometimes I see Ms. Davis looking so worried and I know she's probably thinking about her mom."

He kept forgetting that his darling girl was unbelievably sensitive and caring. Definitely a lot like Maya. He'd have to remember that.

"I wish it wouldn't close, either."

"Is there anything we can do to help?" She bit her lip. Something she always did when nervous.

"I've been wondering, too. Any suggestions?"

"Well...now that you ask, I actually did think of something." Jade sounded so uncertain. "Wasn't going to mention it, but..."

"Let's hear it."

She jumped up.

"I'll do more than that." She ran upstairs to her room and came back with a notebook. Placing it in front of her dad she said, "I have an idea, but I'm not confident about it."

Flicking through the pages, he was surprised at all the writing, numbers and charts. Guess he shouldn't be, since she had done the same when building the stable scene for the pageant. She was definitely meticulous about everything she did.

"Look, honey. I know you're anxious to get riding. How about you leave this with me and I'll spend some time reading it over."

"Okay. Cuz I might need some help to make this happen." She looked nervous. "That is, if you think it'll work."

"I believe you can do anything you put your mind to. I'm proud of you for doing this. Looks like you put a lot of thought into it."

"I did and, oh, that'd be great if you read it."

Once again, she looked anxious. As if she didn't trust him to take her seriously. He couldn't blame her. In the past, he was always brushing her off.

She picked up her dishes and headed to the dishwasher.

"You don't have to do that," he said. "I'll clean up. You go out and have some fun. I don't think you have enough of that."

She looked at him oddly. "Well, okay, Dad. Thanks." She ran over to give him a hug. Something she hadn't done in a while. "You don't mind keeping an eye on Ivy?"

"Not in the least." He glanced down at the happy little pup, snoozing away, her head nestled on a stuffed baby lamb, using it as her pillow. "We've become good friends. And just so you know, as soon as I've cleaned up here, I promise, I'll get right to reading your plans."

Her eyes sparkled as if there were tiny candles inside. They reminded him of the ones he'd seen in the chapel.

"Good," said Jade. "I can't wait to see what you think of my plans. See ya later, Dad." After gently patting her dog on the head, careful not to wake her, she was out the door in minutes.

"Well, it's just you and me, Ivy."

Matt smiled, watching the little dog look up at hearing the door shut, yawn and stumble over to her bed, curling up and falling right back to sleep again. One of her beds. She had at least three of them, in numerous colors and fabrics, scattered throughout the house. She was one spoiled pup and he wouldn't have it any other way.

He cleaned up the kitchen, then, as promised, took Jade's notebook to his office. Settling on his chair, he set the book on his desk and carefully read every word she'd written. Twice. He was amazed at how much work and research she had put into this project.

It was brilliant.

Most of all, it just might work.

Hearing laughter outside the window, he jumped up and looked outside. There was his beautiful daughter riding Gabrielle down a trail leading out of the woods. She seemed to be sharing a joke with the horse, which was not unusual, since she talked to all animals as if they were human. She was an incredible person and she deserved way more than he gave her. Recalling how happy she was at being allowed to sing and dance, he feared he had let her down and that his protection was possibly stifling. He needed to allow her more freedom, not keep her locked in a box. He needed to do more.

Click.

A thought came to mind.

A way of doing something nice for her. Something she'd like.

Should he?

Yes, he should.

He made a decision.

He figured she'd finished her ride and was heading back. He knew exactly what he could do to keep her smiling.

Carefully putting her notebook in a drawer and quickly finishing up a work-related email, he took off to the arena to seek out James, his right-hand man. He found him just finishing up a lesson.

"Would you mind keeping an eye on Ivy for a while?" Matt asked. "I'll put her inside her crate where she'll probably sleep for a good long time, but I'd feel better knowing you'd check her out periodically."

"Not a problem. I'm a dog lover. I'll make sure she's fine."

"Thanks." Next, he went looking for Jade, and found her in the barn, brushing down her horse.

"Good morning again," he said.

"Oh, morning again, Dad." She grinned.

"Enjoy your ride?"

"Loved it."

"So, I was thinking, would you like a ride to church?"

She looked startled.

"Are you serious?"

"Yes, I am."

"Oh, okay. I'd like that. I'm actually done here. Just have to put her back in her stall."

"You go ahead and get ready. I'll finish up."

"Er, okay."

"Meet you out in the car."

She looked puzzled, but ran out fast, probably in case he changed his mind.

"Well, Gabrielle. You look good." He gave her a pat then secured her in her stall and hurried in to change as well. He next placed a sleeping Ivy in her crate, then went out to start the car.

In a few minutes, Jade came out the front door. She had changed into a dress and had on her good coat and boots and it struck him hard that she was growing up fast. She was not that little kid anymore who used to follow him around. When had she gotten so tall, he wondered?

"Did you look at my plans to save the bakery?" she asked, sliding into her seat.

"Yes, I did, and I'm impressed." He turned down the driveway to the road.

"You are?" Her voice rose in pitch.

"I am." He glanced over at her. "Why do you sound so surprised? It's a good proposal. You put a lot of thought into it."

She touched his arm. "I care, Dad."

"I know you do."

"Do you think it might work?"

"I do. It's ambitious, but you have figured out solutions to every possible scenario. It's a good plan and I'll help you all I can."

"Thanks. I counted on it. Pinky swear?"

He laughed when she stuck her baby finger up beside the wheel when they were stopped at a red light. She used to do that all the time as a kid to cement promises. He was happy to see this little girl behavior still there.

Touching her finger briefly with his, he said, "Pinky swear. And by the way, you look lovely today."

"Thanks."

He shot a quick look at her. She seemed pleased.

Finally getting a green light, he drove down the road and turned into the parking lot of the church. He pulled to a stop.

"Oh, Dad. You could have just let me off at the front door."

"No, I couldn't." He got out and held the car door for her.

"What are you doing?"

He smiled. "I'm going with you."

"You're coming in, too?"

"Yes, I am."

"But what about Ivy?"

"James is babysitting her."

"Oh."

So excited, she grabbed his hand and they walked in together. Once again, she hadn't done that in years and he was astounded at how proud and thrilled she looked. And to think, he had denied her all of this.

Immediately he spotted Serena coming towards them. Jade had mentioned she was a greeter at the church and guess she was in the choir as well, because she wore a long blue robe which set her hair afire. Their eyes locked and she looked surprised.

"Hi, Ms. Davis," Jade said.

"Well, hello there."

"Look. Dad came with me." Jade practically bobbed up and down.

"I see that."

"What are you singing today?"

"Mostly Christmas carols."

"Um, can I join them, Dad? Please?"

Of course, she would want to. He should have thought of that. She used to sing in the choir with her mother.

"Yes, you can. Go ahead."

"Are you okay sitting alone?"

"Hey, I'm used to it. Remember?" He smiled.

"Thanks," mouthed Serena.

He chose a seat at the back and looked around. Although he'd attended rehearsals in the auditorium, he hadn't stepped inside the actual church section where the congregation gathered to pray. He had been in the small chapel attached to the hall, but that was it. He also hadn't attended a service in a very long time, not since Maya's funeral. When he went to school here in Angel, he used to attend this very same church with his folks. Surprisingly, it looked the same. Same pictures, same burning candles.

He started to feel uncomfortable, almost panicky.

Churches made him face things, and he wasn't sure he wanted to.

As the choir took its place, he curbed the impulse to run out the door, and settled down to watch his daughter. She was all smiles and he felt ashamed he had stopped her from doing this over the past two years.

He was still mad at God, just not as much, and still felt unworthy.

He'd deal with that later. For now, it was all about his daughter and her joy at being in the choir.

His flood of emotions could wait until he was ready to deal with them.

If ever.

Twenty-two

Serena found herself staring at Matt all through the service.

It didn't help that the choir was situated on risers back behind the altar area, so they were always facing the congregation.

Oh, she tried to disguise it, taking breaks here and there, but mostly she was mesmerized.

Just why did he have to constantly wear plaid shirts? And why did she have to like that particular style?

Of course, she knew why.

It was what her dad had worn all the time.

She had oodles of memories as a kid snuggling up on her dad's lap, burying her nose in the soft warm plaid. When he passed away, she had kept one of his shirts, tucking it under her pillow, comforting her, making her feel safe. Eventually, she grew big enough to wear it, and it became her go-to in times of sadness. It was warm and familiar and wrapping it around her bolstered her way back to hope again. In college, her friends used to tease her, saying they always knew what she felt when she had it on. After all these years, she still kept it hanging in her closet, ready to pull on whenever the need arose.

It seemed unbelievable that Matt wore a similar shirt often, just in different colors. Of course, many people wore those shirts...after all, they were incredibly comfortable, but Matt seemed to have one on all the time, almost as if it were a uniform. Funny how it heightened her attraction to him and drew her towards him, despite her heart protesting big-time. Oh, it wasn't that he represented a father figure to her; it was just the shirt signaled comfort, love, warmth. And trust. Something she had struggled with after her last disastrous relationship.

She just hoped he didn't notice her constant focus on him, but he seemed fixated on his daughter, so that was to her benefit.

She was still stunned he was actually here, sitting in the church, and she knew it had to be his love for Jade that got him to go. He was letting her sing both at the pageant and now in the choir. Sounded like he was changing, or at least listening to his daughter.

Watching him smile at Jade, her heart raced as, unbidden, all sorts of cozy feelings swarmed her. She had always thought he was a nice guy. Yes, they'd had a falling-out as kids in elementary school, but his latest actions had moved her.

Don't think about him.

Stop it.

She closed her eyes.

Dear God, help me to not think about Matt.

Wait. What?

Oh, no.

Big mistake. Big, big mistake.

Never close your eyes when standing on a riser in front of the whole church.

Disoriented, she began to wobble back and forth, then suddenly tumbled down, just managing to stop herself from landing on her backside. She attributed her quick save to her ballet training and flexibility.

Hurry. Right yourself, then get back on that step fast.

Maybe no one noticed.

Yeah, right.

Several choir members were staring at her in horror, not to mention Jade's shocked look.

Had Matt seen her?

She sneaked a glance. Judging by his eyebrows soaring to the ceiling, he had.

The choir swung into another song.

Act like everything is all right. Concentrate on the songs and Jade's joy in being part of the choir.

With the young girl's pure voice, they sounded so much better. Amazing that she was able to harmonize simply by listening and pure instinct. She had such innate talent; the type all the training in the world couldn't produce. She had the so-called 'it' factor that made her stand out.

Serena wobbled again.

Stop it.

Pay attention.

Couldn't believe she'd actually fallen—literally fallen—all because she was trying not to think about Matt. If she didn't watch out, it would happen again.

Forget about my fall.

Forget about Matt.

At least God answered her prayer, she thought, almost breaking into a giggle. Teetering on a riser made her stop focusing solely on Matt. But it didn't help that the sermon was all about love and giving and the spirit of Christmas, which made her think of him again. Sigh.

She glanced at him for about the fiftieth time. It also bothered her that his hair was falling into his eyes as usual and she wanted to rush over and brush it back. Seemed like she was starting to like him. A lot. Way too much.

She had no time for that.

So, she upped her praying like she always did, for the bakery to be saved. That was her main focus. It had to be, and she needed no distractions.

She couldn't resist his magnetism, however. Frustrating as it was.

After the service, she found herself walking right over to him. Just couldn't help it.

"Thanks again for letting Jade sing at the pageant and now in the choir. She seems to love it."

"She does." He looked serious. "Are you okay? Did you fall up there?"

"Nah. Just slipped a little." But her red face gave away her embarrassment.

"Dad, Dad. How did the choir sound?"

Saved again by his daughter's arrival. Saved from possible explanations about her tumbling episode.

She saw his eyes warm at his daughter's happy face and obvious joy.

"Did you have a good time, honey?"

"I had a great time. But hey, can we go to the bakery, Dad? Please?" begged Jade.

"I guess." He looked at Serena. "You don't mind, do you?"

"Daddy, it's a store. Anyone can go."

"And of course, I don't mind," Serena said. "I'll meet you there."

"Would you like a ride?" asked Matt.

"No, no. The walk will do me good."

And get me focused, she hoped.

She took off fast, struggling to rein herself in and put an end to falling for him. She needed to pull herself back from that edge. She could do that. She had once already and could do it again. Sure, she had been a little kid back then and it had hurt, but it'd be faster as an adult and pain free.

Yes, she could do it.

Entering the bakery, Serena waved to her mother, then quickly ran up to her apartment, tossing off her coat and boots. She slipped off her dress, pulled on a t-shirt, tugged on her jeans, slid into comfortable flats and threw on her apron. She ran back down the stairs to the kitchen and had the Jenkinses' coffee, hot chocolate and cinnamon buns ready the minute they walked in the door.

"Would you like to join us?" asked Matt, as she led them to a table.

"Thanks, but no. I have work to do."

Did he seem disappointed? She eyed him, squinting. Well, maybe a little. But she just couldn't allow anyone or anything to weaken her focus. Besides, it was probably wishful thinking assuming he was upset she couldn't join them.

Concentrate on Jade instead.

"Here's an extra cookie," she said with a wink. "Actually a few extra." She handed over a bag. "For later."

Jade grinned. "Thanks. Guess what?"

"I give up. What?" She loved the fact that Jade's dimples burst out whenever she was happy.

"We got our tree yesterday."

"You did? That's exciting."

"Yes, it is. We're going to decorate it this afternoon, before we come back to town tonight for Light Up Night. Hey, I have an idea. Dad, can Ms. Davis come over and help us decorate?"

Oh, no. This was exactly what Serena didn't want. She couldn't afford to get involved any more than she already was.

"Well, okay, if she's not too busy," Matt said.

He didn't sound thrilled about the idea, but probably didn't want to let his daughter down.

"Oh, thanks," Serena said quickly. "That's a nice gesture, but I'm too busy."

"Go ahead, honey," her mom called out, coming out of the kitchen, obviously overhearing what Jade had said. "It's time you have some fun."

Oh, no.

"Please?" begged Jade. "You can even taste the cookies I made last night. Not as good as yours, but they have lots of sprinkles on them."

"Well, I can't resist that and I bet they're delicious. Okay then. I'll come." She just couldn't say no to Jade's happy face.

"And bring Holly, too."

She looked at Matt.

"No problem, of course your dog can join us."

"Yeah, and we better go now," Jade said, checking her watch. "I need to get home to Ivy. She needs to learn to be on her own, but I don't like leaving her too long. James is watching out for her, but I'm sure she's wondering where I am."

Surprisingly, she jumped up and gave Serena a hug. "See ya soon, Ms. Davis."

"Okay. I'll be there."

After they left, Serena started to help Mary clean up.

"You go ahead, honey. I'm okay here."

"No way will I leave you with all these dishes."

"Oh, don't worry. Go. If you don't, they'll be finished that tree before you get there. Besides, you said yes and they're expecting you."

Serena placed her hands on her hips and tried to summon up a stern look. "As I recall, you were the one who volunteered me to go."

"Well, it's time you had some fun."

"I do have fun."

Her mom grinned. "Well, go have some more. And maybe dress up a little. Or at least get out of those jeans."

"But I always wear jeans, except when I'm at church or teaching."

"Well, it might be nice to put on something different for a change. Something bright showing a little Christmas spirit. Now get going. You're going to miss it all."

"All right. All right. I'll go. After all, I did promise."

Serena took off her apron and ran up the stairs to her apartment.

Twenty-three

Maybe her mother had a point.

Serena was originally just going to run over to the Jenkinses' wearing what she had on, jeans and a tee. That was, until she realized she had dollops of flour and cookie dough stuck to her clothes in hard little clumps, impossible to scrape off.

She stood in front of her wardrobe, realizing it was filled with jeans and more jeans. Tees and more tees.

I don't really care, she thought.

But maybe she should.

Oh, she knew her mother's motive. It was to have her dress up, secretly hoping she'd find a serious boyfriend. It was true, though, she usually dressed in dark colors, but here in a town that shouted the joy of Christmas everywhere you looked, it might be good for her to get in the spirit. Especially when Christmas tree decorating with a young girl who was thrilled about the event.

She would never dress to look good for a man. Not her style. Dressing to suit herself was what she believed in. But a little Christmas brightness wouldn't hurt.

Reaching into the back of her closet, she pulled out a pair of red corduroy pants and a soft green sweater that apparently made her hair and eyes pop. Or so her college friend Martha always said. Whatever that meant. She quickly changed out of her bakery wear and tied her hair back with a bright red ribbon.

She looked in the mirror.

Red and green colors.

She couldn't look more in the Christmas spirit.

Now off to see Jade. And Matt.

Her stomach twisted.

A wave of confusion rippled through her.

Maybe she shouldn't go. Being around him unsettled her.

She sat on the edge of the bed.

Should she?

She didn't need distractions right about now. She needed to keep focused on the bakery, school and the pageant. Anything else would be an interference. Especially Matt and his plaid shirts.

The door opened and Holly came racing up the stairs, jumped on her lap and started licking her face.

"Guess Mom told you to come find me, right?"

Holly peered at her, trying to figure out what she was saying, tail wagging.

"Bet you'd love to go visiting."

Holly licked her face.

"Guess we should." Serena laughed at how excited Holly was. Going out was her favorite thing to do. "Besides, it's too late now to back out, since I promised Jade. All right. C'mon." She took one last look in the mirror, decided she looked okay, and went back down to the bakery.

"You look lovely, dear," her mom said, hurrying out of the kitchen as if she had been listening for her arrival. Probably to make sure Serena went. "Bright and cheery."

"Thanks, Mom."

"Here. Why don't you wear these?"

Serena glanced down at her mother's hand.

"Your rose earrings?"

They were Mary's prized possession, gifted by her husband on the last Christmas they had spent together. Her dad had found them in a jewelry shop and, knowing how much his wife loved roses, bought them. They were beautiful, made of gold, delicate, exquisite and memorable, just like Mary, he always said. She treasured them and only wore them on special occasions and had never before offered them to Serena.

"They'll look lovely on you."

"Well, okay." She certainly couldn't refuse such a beautiful offering, so she quickly took out the hoop earrings she was wearing and inserted the rose ones.

She looked in the mirror on the wall by the counter.

"They look nice on you," her mom said.

They really did. But they'd look nice on anyone, they were so gorgeous.

"This Matt guy. He seems like quite a gentleman," she added.

"Don't get any ideas, Mom." Serena turned to look at her. "I'm not in the market for a romance."

Her mother winked.

"You never know. Have a good time."

"Hopefully I will. But you get those stars out of your eyes. I know what you're trying to do."

Serena burst out laughing as she reached out to hug her grinning mother. Mary would love nothing more than to have her daughter married off with her first grandchild on the way. Good luck with that. Serena was still in her early thirties and in no rush.

"Thanks for letting me wear them. I'll take good care of them."

"I know you will."

Serena snapped on Holly's leash and off they went.

The whole drive over, she blared the radio, trying to drown out thoughts of chickening out, turning around the car and heading back home. Her fingers touched her borrowed earrings, searching for courage. No, she had to keep going. A promise is a promise, she kept repeating over and over. Besides, her mother would be disappointed.

So she kept driving, eventually pulling into the farm. After all, she did love decorating a Christmas tree. It was one of her favorite things to do with her mother.

Pulling to a stop, reluctantly but now a tad excited and anticipating some fun, she let Holly out of the car and they knocked on the door. Or really, she knocked, Holly barked.

Jade opened the door holding Ivy.

"Oh, goody, you came. Hi, Holly."

Holly beamed up at her, sat and raised her paw for a shake. Jade leaned down and obliged her.

"She's so sweet. Come on in."

They did, while little Ivy squeaked her delight. "Guess she wants down to play with Holly," Jade said.

She put the pup on the floor and Serena smiled at how adorable they looked together with Holly nuzzling Ivy and the wee pup staring adoringly at Holly. At least her dog was happy they'd come.

Matt came out to the foyer, of course wearing a blue plaid flannel shirt. "Here, let me take your coat."

She felt shy seeing him, instantly reliving their almost kisses, and wondered if her eyes reflected her interest. She hoped not.

He led them into the living room. Serena stifled a laugh at how Holly kept glancing back and forth between Matt and Ivy, not clear what to do. Seemed she liked them both and didn't know which one to fawn over.

She stopped in her tracks when she noticed the tree.

"Wow. Absolutely gorgeous," she exclaimed. And it was. Tall, bushy and mighty, taking up almost a whole wall.

"We cut it down ourselves," Jade said proudly.

"You did a good job. It's magnificent."

"Almost didn't get it in the house." Matt chuckled. "But with lots of twisting and turning, we made it."

"It's perfect."

It was. Getting even more excited, Serena looked around at the boxes labeled "Decorations."

"You certainly have a lot of ornaments," she said. "Which are well needed, considering the size of the tree."

"Yes. Most are Mom's." She dropped her voice to a whisper. "Dad thought we should get new ones, but I love all of them. Brings back good memories."

Serena wondered if it was painful for Matt to see them, but Jade looked like she was raring to get started.

"Well, time to dig in," Matt said. "We want to be on time for the Christmas gathering tonight."

"We string the lights on first, right, Dad?" asked Jade. "Are they ready to go?"

"They are. I'll get them." He left the room briefly and came back with an armload of bulbs attached by wire. "I spent part of the morning testing them to make sure they all work and fortunately they do."

Jade grabbed one end, Matt the other, and Serena took hold of the middle section, as round and round the tree they went, carefully placing the bulbs over and under the branches.

"Good," Jade said, standing back observing their work. "Now, on to the ornaments."

Serena glanced over to see if the pup was okay. No problem there, Holly was on guard, watching over Ivy and keeping her safe. Good girl.

They all started opening boxes.

"Here are my favorite ones." Matt picked up a paper snowflake equipped with a pipe cleaner to loop around a branch. He placed it carefully and next added a crayoned Christmas tree and a sweet clothespin reindeer.

"You're not serious, Dad! I forgot about those. You're still going to hang all the ones I made when I was little?"

"Yes. They're the best of the bunch."

Jade looked embarrassed as her dad proceeded to carefully place on the tree home-made cardboard candy canes, a play dough Santa and multiple construction paper snowflakes. Serena loved how they had all been gently wrapped in thick paper to prevent damage, courtesy probably of Matt and his wife.

He stood back, pride just beaming from him.

"See? They're beautiful, Jade," he said.

And Serena's heart melted at the warmth in his eyes.

"They are," she added.

"Well, okay then." Jade threw up her arms. "Guess they'll do."

Serena noticed that even though protesting, Jade seemed happy about them, after all.

And as for Matt...she'd been trying to stay clear of him the whole time, hard to do in such a small space. Their fingers had touched a few times while reaching for ornaments and her breath had quickened. She kept her eyes down, not wanting him to see, still figuring they'd give away her feelings. She also kept turning her attention to Jade, who had a great time as she sang and danced around them, taking the dogs out for a potty break, then coming back and offering her a cookie and eggnog every few seconds. After three, she had to finally say no.

"They're absolutely delicious, but I can't eat any more. I'm stuffed, but I sure would love the recipe."

"You like them?"

She looked thrilled.

"Like them? I love them," Serena said, happy to see Jade's smile grow wider. "Your creativity shines in the way you made an original Christmas scene on each cookie with sprinkles, gumdrops and licorice. They're amazing."

"Well, thanks. I was inspired by you. I've seen some of the cookies you've decorated."

"And now I'm inspired by you."

"I just hope you saved room for pizza."

"Pizza?"

"Yeah, that's what we're having for supper. You can stay, right?"

"Well..."

"Please."

"Oh, okay."

She wasn't sure it was a good idea to stay. Eating together was way too intimate, but gave in to the girl's excitement. Plus the dogs were curled up together and she would hate interrupting their nap.

Or at least that was what she told herself. In fact, she didn't want to leave. She was having a good time.

"Looks like we're done," Jade said, hanging the last ornament.

"I agree." Serena stood back to take in the whole tree brimming with color, all glowing and shiny. It was spectacular.

"Just one final step," Matt said. He carried over a gold box and placed it on the coffee table.

"It's the angel," Jade said. "Mom's angel. Can I do it, Dad? Can I put it on top?"

"Of course you can."

Matt went into the kitchen and came out with a small step ladder. "Up you go," he said.

Carefully taking the angel out of its box, Jade climbed up the ladder and gently placed it on top. She scooted back down and stood there staring at it.

"Mom found it at a flea market," she said. "And fell in love with it."

Serena could see why. It was magnificent. Long blonde hair, flowing white robe, lacy wings and the most peaceful face Serena had ever seen on a tree topper. It looked a lot like Jade.

"Now the moment we've all been waiting for," Matt said dramatically. "Drum roll, please."

Jade hit the ladder in a rhythmic beat as her dad plugged in the lights.

They all clapped as pops of white light danced around the tree, highlighting the decorations by ensuring they sparkled. Even the dogs woke up and pranced around, probably assuming they were the reason for the applause.

"Now, pizza," Jade said, clearly enjoying herself.

Expecting it to be ordered in, when they all trooped into the kitchen, Serena was surprised to discover that Matt had made the pizzas.

"You even made your own dough?"

"Sure did. I actually like to cook," he said, pulling them out of the oven where he'd obviously been keeping them warm. "Not saying I'm good at it. But I enjoy it. Definitely not much of a baker, though."

"He's even teaching me stuff," Jade said proudly, placing a sleeping Ivy on her bed. Holly yawned and curled up beside her. "I can make a pretty good lasagna. I'll have to make it for you some day."

"Looking forward to it." She wasn't, though. Matt was too much distraction for her to handle and being around him confused her. On the other hand, she'd hate to refuse the generosity of this young girl.

The pizza was delicious.

Lots of cheese, veggies and pepperoni, heightened further by fun, amiable conversation.

Taking her last bite, Jade said, "Will you be at Light Up Night in town? We're going shortly. It'll be my first one here in Angel. Dad went to them when he was a kid."

Serena glanced at her watch. "I didn't realize it was so late. Yes, I'll be there with my mother. I don't think I've ever missed one."

"It sounds cool. Dad said the whole town comes out and the mayor leads us in singing 'Jingle Bells' and then he plugs in the lights for the tree."

"That's right. And by the way, your tree is pretty much the same size as the town's tree."

"I bet you're right." Jade laughed. "Hey, how about we meet you there?"

"Sure." Serena nodded. "Sounds like a good plan."

It meant she had to see Matt again, which left her both excited and not so thrilled, all at the same time. She just couldn't think of a fast excuse, especially since she had just told Jade she'd be there.

After helping with the dishes, or in fact just throwing the fancy Christmas paper plates in the recycling bin, she decided it was time to leave. Jade was busy feeding Ivy, who was awake from her nap, so Matt walked her to the door carrying Holly, who had decided she needed to spend some time with their host after all. She had whined and barked to get his attention and looked quite pleased she'd won.

"Thank you for dropping over. Jade appreciated it."

He didn't?

"She's a delightful young girl."

"Yes, she is. I don't deserve her."

"Yes, you do."

She shivered as he helped her on with her coat and even pulled her hair out over her collar. Sad to say, the romantic books she scoffed at were right again. He set her pulse racing. Quickly leashing Holly, she took off at a run to her car.

Smiling all the way home, still immersed in the fun she'd just experienced, she parked, got out, and unhooked Holly from her seatbelt. She quickly joined her mother and Gloria to walk over to the park, which was just down the street.

"How'd it go?" asked Mary.

"Okay."

"Just okay? Come on, I want details."

"Ms. Davis! Ms. Davis!"

Serena turned to see Jade bearing down on her. They must have left right after she had. Good. Now, she wouldn't have to answer her mom's question.

The girl started to run, Matt behind her holding Ivy. The sight of that big man carrying the little dog so tenderly made her heart hurt.

Once again, she faced the fact she cared way too much.

She hoped her mom wasn't watching her, for she would know in a minute, always able to read Serena's facial expressions. She looked around. Her mother seemed to have given up on her, as she chatted with Sunny and Helen off to the right. She'd lucked out.

Jade seemed happy as she grabbed her dad's hand and then reached out to take hers, and they made their way to the gigantic Christmas tree. Serena glanced back, checking on her mother, and saw her wink and wave her on. There were those stars in her eyes again. She'd be knitting baby blankets if Serena didn't make her see this romance was not going to happen. Ever.

Enough of that.

Every few seconds she found herself greeting students, colleagues, customers of the bakery. The event signaled the true beginning of this joyful season and was always a fun time.

"Oh, Dad, can I go get some hot chocolate?"

Serena was glad of the interruption, since her thoughts were all over the place.

"Sure. Go ahead."

"Great. I'll bring some back for all of us." She ran over to the refreshment table.

"Seems like moving here has been good for her," Serena said, watching her chatting with other students in her class as she lined up for drinks.

"I hope so. She appears more content these days."

"I've also noticed she is making a lot of friends in class."

"Good. Glad to hear that."

He put down a squirming Ivy who wanted to be near Holly. The two of them walked together, one on a blue leash, the other a pink one.

"And thank you again for letting her sing. You'll be amazed when you see how she transforms the pageant."

"I'm looking forward to it. I think it's been good for her, judging by how enthusiastic she's been." He paused for a second, then said, "Any luck with saving Petals?"

"Not yet."

Jade stopped them from a further chat and possible tears on Serena's side by arriving back with the hot chocolate. The possibility of losing the bakery always made her emotional and her eyes glistened. Thankfully, she was distracted by noticing Nancy waving at her from the other side of the park. Was she with Nick? She squinted. Yes, she was. That was sure interesting. She'd have to get the scoop later.

After a rousing and very offkey rendition of "Jingle Bells," the countdown to the tree lighting began, as Mayor John Sachs shouted, "Three... two... one..."

Jade slid out between them to move closer and Serena and Matt's hands accidentally touched. She was reluctant to move hers away. It also crossed her mind that Jade might be doing a bit of matchmaking. But surely, she imagined that.

As the tree lit up and everyone oohed and aahed, it was all she could do to stop her hand from curling around his.

Yep, she was in big time like with this guy.

Totally against her will.

Twenty-four

Matt found it hard to concentrate on the brief he was drafting. As usual, his thoughts were full of Serena. Her smiles as they decorated the tree, her warm eyes as they enjoyed the town light-up night, her laughter when his daughter's delight made the two of them chuckle and of course, the brief moments when their hands touched. Seemed like everything she did left a huge impact on him. Again. Just like when he was a kid. Except now he was an adult and it disturbed him.

As usual, he always seemed to be running toward and away from her at the same time.

Did he want another relationship? Did he deserve one? Would he do to Serena what he had done to his wife? Make promises but not follow through?

He'd married when he was young. Twenty seemed like a kid these days. They'd met during their first week of college, spent all their time together, and he'd felt it was the right step. Looking back, he realized he had not been mature enough and focused way too much on getting into law school and then, of course, his job was all consuming. Or he made it so, equating monetary rewards with success. Now he realized being a good husband and father was his true measure of happiness.

The last thing he wanted was to ever hurt Maya.

But he had. And he would have to live with that pain all his life.

He couldn't do that to Serena. He needed to stay away from her, but he still wanted to see her.

Distracted, he reached over and picked up the flyer Jade had left on his desk announcing the pageant. His eyes centered on the date for the first time.

December twenty-third.

Oh no.

It was the exact anniversary of his wife's death. Two years ago.

A day Matt dreaded.

Come on. It was the same date? Couldn't be.

He stared at the printed words and letters, willing them to disappear or change somehow.

They didn't.

Odd how he hadn't paid much attention to the actual date of the pageant, just knew it was happening sometime in December. Of course, he knew it was near Christmas Day, but hadn't thought much about it or glanced at the flyer until now.

His heart sank.

It seemed ominous that his daughter was performing her first solo on the anniversary of her mother's death. His hands shook as he dropped the piece of paper back on his desk.

Reality sliced through him.

All last year, he had ignored this date.

Avoided it.

Kept busy.

He never mentioned it.

Neither did Jade.

He wasn't sure if she was silent because she followed his lead, or just forgot about or ignored it.

Or couldn't face it, just like him.

And he never asked, simply not wanting to deal with his own emotions or Jade's. Another failure of his. Hiding feelings was the wrong thing to do. He knew, but did it anyway.

The fact Jade was singing on this exact date upset him to no end.

Fears twisted and tossed as his mind raced.

One fact rose to the forefront.

He was wrong.

He shouldn't have allowed Jade to sing. He should have stuck to his decision to protect her and not open her up to unwanted attention.

Possibly deadly attention.

He couldn't let it happen again. He had failed his wife; he couldn't fail Jade. There were too many copycat stalkers out there who would take pure joy in going after his daughter. Make a name for themselves in a sick fashion. For all he knew, his wife's stalker could even reach out from jail and cause a huge problem. Get the daughter because he couldn't get the mother.

Who could possibly guess what could happen? His mind twirled like a kaleidoscope he once had as a kid, over and over, spinning out of control, horrible scenarios flashing before his eyes.

He couldn't fail her like he had failed Maya.

He just couldn't.

The door opened. Ivy barked her excitement.

Jade was home.

"How was school?" he asked, coming out of his office to greet her.

"Great." Her eyes sparkled and she looked happy.

Too bad he had to burst her bubble.

"Would you like a snack? I picked up some of those cinnamon buns you like."

"Great. From Petals?"

"Yes, from Petals. When you're ready, come on out to the kitchen."

"Sure, Dad. Just want to drop my books up on my desk."

He hurried to the fridge, poured milk and placed a bun on a plate.

After a few minutes, Jade came racing in, Ivy following right behind as usual.

"So, is school going okay?" he asked, joining her at the table.

"Yes, finally. I'm making lots of friends. Sure don't feel so lonely anymore."

"That's wonderful. And how is the pageant coming along?"

"Much better."

He had to do it. Now. He had to keep her safe.

"Well, honey, I need to talk to you about something."

"Oh, okay. Go ahead."

"I won't sugar-coat it. I can't let you sing."

"Pardon?" Her mouth dropped in shock. Her face reddened.

Matt's heart softened, but his urge to protect her was too strong.

"I just can't do it, honey. I can't let you sing 'O Holy Night.'"

"But Dad, I've been practicing and practicing and practicing. I've been over at the hall every day during lunch hour getting used to the microphone. I have to sing. The pageant is counting on me."

"I'm sorry honey. It's too dangerous."

"Because of what happened to Mom?"

"Yes."

"Because it's on the same date as when she died?"

"You remember that?"

"Of course, I do."

"Why haven't you mentioned it?"

"Because you never do. And I don't want to upset you."

"Oh." It was all he could think of to say. He had failed her. He should be the one looking out for her, not the other way around.

"Please. Can't you change your mind? Please, Dad?"

"Sorry. No."

She jumped up from the table. "Well, I'm going to go groom Gabrielle. C'mon, Ivy."

"Don't you want to finish your snack?" The fact Jade left food on her plate was a shocker.

"Nope, not hungry."

She raced to the door, threw on her coat and boots, leashed up Ivy and was gone in minutes.

He was left staring into space.

Did I do the right thing?

He wasn't sure. Especially seeing how upset he had made her.

Doubts crowded and filled his thoughts. He knew Jade wouldn't like his decision, but he had hoped she'd understand.

An image of God flew through his thoughts.

Should he pray?

Somehow, he couldn't bring himself to do so. He had let God down so many times, why would He even listen to him now? Especially after he pulled his daughter from a Christmas pageant honoring Jesus' birth.

Should he run after Jade? Make sure she was okay?

No. She probably needed space.

Instead he busied himself preparing for supper, pulling out a frozen lasagna he'd made the week before. It was one of her favorite meals, that and garlic bread. Sticking it in the oven, he hurried to his office to finish up some work. The buzzer signaling supper was ready rang out just as he completed his last email. Shutting down his computer, he went back to the kitchen to get everything ready.

He glanced at the clock.

No Jade.

Usually she was there right at five-thirty, an agreed upon time. They always ate at the exact same moment every day.

Where was she?

He called her. No answer. Texted. No answer.

At six o'clock, he walked over to the barn.

Gabrielle was in her stall, groomed, and happily eating away.

No Jade. No Ivy.

He saw James.

"Have you seen my daughter around?" he asked.

"No, sorry, I haven't. I've been in the arena with a student. Just came back here to pick up my camera. Why, is she missing?"

"No. Not at all. Just wanted to tell her something."

James gave him a quizzical look as he walked back to the arena.

Matt's heart pounded.

Had she fallen somewhere? Hurt herself?

"Jade! Ivy!" he yelled.

No answer.

He checked all through the barn, peeking in every stall.

Nothing.

Racing outside, he looked around the yard.

Nothing.

He hurried back into the house.

"Jade? Ivy?"

Not a sound.

He knocked at her bedroom door. Maybe she had slipped in and he hadn't noticed.

"Are you in there, honey?"

No response.

He slowly opened the door to her room.

She wasn't there.

Panic flared. Exploded. His mind filled with what ifs...

Sure she was upset, but she wouldn't leave, would she?

Would his daughter actually run away?

Take off some place?

Hurrying to the kitchen, he turned off the oven and headed outside for the second time.

He started to search the fields behind the house, shining his flashlight back and forth, stopping every few minutes to call her name. She rarely ventured in this direction during a school night, but one never knew.

And then he saw them.

Small human footprints and tiny dog prints.

Jade and Ivy.

He followed the prints into the woods, glad of the snow that showed them clearly.

Eventually there were only Jade's steps. Guess she was carrying Ivy at that point.

A path snaked through a clumping of trees which led to the downtown area of Angel. The footprints were still evident until he hit the streets. Then they stopped, mainly because the sidewalks were shoveled, and nothing could be seen.

Looking up and down the main core of the town, he wondered where she'd go.

Most important, was she safe?

Twenty-five

"Good, that's finished," Serena muttered to herself as she walked into the café from the kitchen. She had just mixed up a batch of buns and slid them into the oven. The timer was set to let her know when they were done and she'd even gotten a new one that was loud and shrill, so no way could she miss it. She couldn't afford to have anything burn again.

She was the only one at Petals...her mother was off shopping, and Helen was making a delivery. The bell signaling customers was silent, or at least she didn't hear it, but figured she'd better check to see if there were any out there. Looking around, she was surprised to see someone off in the corner, slumped over, head down. She quickly walked over.

"Excuse me, may I help you?" she asked.

Much to her shock, Jade looked up. Tears rolled down her cheeks and she held Ivy in her arms as if the pup were her only friend. Serena was alarmed at how sad she appeared.

"Oh, honey, what's wrong?"

The girl sniffed. "Just about everything, but sorry, is it okay that Ivy is with me?"

"Sure. But let's go into the back so you can have some privacy."

She glanced at the clock. Her mother would be here soon if any customers showed up.

She led the girl to the dogs' room and pulled out two folding chairs.

"Please, take a seat."

Serena sat as well. Gloria stared at Ivy with interest, especially when Holly ran over to greet the pup. All of them wagged their tails in anticipation of some fun playtime.

Jade watched them for a while, tears still streaming down her face. Growing increasingly alarmed, Serena finally leaned over and said softly, "Jade, what's wrong."

She sobbed for a few more minutes, then finally looked up. "Dad won't let me sing at the pageant."

Immediately, Serena could feel a headache surface and begin pounding away.

Oh, no.

"Not at all?"

"No. He said he can't risk it. Especially since the pageant is on the same date as Mom's death. Guess he didn't realize that until now."

As upset as Serena was, because of course it would affect the play and a possible job, somehow in the depths of her heart, she couldn't blame him. She had read more of his wife's story just last night and it was heart-wrenching. She had also realized the date of his wife's death was the same as the pageant, but figured he had known that when he'd agreed to let her sing. It must have all been just too painful for him when he found out, and she understood why singing on the exact anniversary date would also be alarming.

"It's okay," Serena said.

"But I'm letting you down."

"No, you're not. I understand. He's just trying to protect you."

"But I want to sing."

"I know. But your dad is very worried about you."

"It's not fair. I'm letting everyone else down, too."

"No, you're not. Please don't think that. Everyone will understand."

"But I really want to sing, Ms. Davis. As my mom always said, 'Singing is a special way to honor God'."

Serena's heart broke at the pain in Jade's eyes.

"I know you do, and your mother was a very wise woman."

"I miss her, you know." She scraped her chair closer. "Dad said you lost your father when you were young, too."

"He's right, I did."

"Do you miss him a lot?"

"Yes, I do. Every single day."

"Me, too." Jade's hand reached out to hold Serena's. "And thanks for not saying stuff like, *they're always with you*, or *they live on in you*. I know that, but I've heard it too often. Thanks for just being here with me."

One thing Serena knew from losing a parent so young was that what had helped her the most were the people who accepted her grief and let her feel it. They didn't try to fix it.

They sat in silence.

Serena held on tight, touched that Jade had reached out to her. She hoped her own strength could flow into this young girl and ease her pain even a small amount.

"Ms. Davis, I just wish my dad would understand how important singing is to me."

"He will one day. Right now, he's afraid of losing you."

"Guess I do know that. But he can't keep me in a box forever."

No, he couldn't.

Pause.

Reality set in.

"How did you get here, by the way?" asked Serena.

"I just took off."

Oh, oh. She should have figured that out.

"Does your dad know where you are?"

"Um, no."

"Guess we better call him. He'll be worried."

"Yeah, I probably shouldn't have taken off so fast."

At that precise moment, as if underscoring Serena's worried comment, she heard loud stomping footsteps and glanced over to the door.

Matt stormed in.

"Serena, are you back here? Sorry to barge in but..."

He looked around, saw Jade and hurried over.

"Are you all right?" he asked.

"Yes, I'm okay."

"Oh, thank goodness." He pulled her into his arms.

Serena could almost see the relief pouring off him.

"How did you find me?" asked Jade.

"I followed your footprints through the woods. I've been looking in every store. I should have thought of Petals first."

"Oh."

Releasing her, Matt stood up. "Please go wait in the café, Jade. I need to talk to Ms. Davis alone for a minute."

Serena wondered why, especially since he sounded so serious. Probably to thank her for keeping his daughter safe. Maybe?

After Jade left Matt turned, locking eyes with her. "How dare you not tell me that she was here? I've been worried sick. You were completely irresponsible." He said each word slowly, pausing for effect.

"But..."

He turned and left, not giving Serena a chance to explain what had happened and that she had been on the verge of calling.

His face haunted her.

He was pale and his eyes were wide with worry.

She had never seen him this upset, nor so angry.

He blamed her completely.

Totally unfair, but justifiable. He had been concerned for Jade and lashed out at her as the nearest target.

She wondered if he'd ever forgive her.

Twenty-six

I'm not going to let Matt's anger get to me. I'm not going to let it get to me.

Sigh.

It's getting to me, thought Serena.

She headed into their last rehearsal before the big event the next day, still upset that Matt was angry with her and blaming her for everything. Here she had tried to be compassionate to his daughter, but he hadn't even given her a chance to explain what had happened.

How dare he.

Obviously, she would have called him and let him know where Jade was, but she hadn't enough time. She was just trying to listen to his daughter, find out what was wrong, and hadn't realized she'd taken off from home without telling her father. Serena had been too worried about what had caused the young girl's tears. Too bad he couldn't have stayed long enough to hear her side.

Mostly she was sad.

Sad for a young girl who wanted to sing for God and a father who was so full of fear.

Sad also about her mother and Petals.

Without Jade singing "O Holy Night," the bakery was doomed.

The taped music didn't cut it, the pageant was still a mess of errors even though they'd improved quite a bit, and she figured she wouldn't get the job now. After all, there would be many qualified teachers applying and her flop of a nativity scene would place her last or even completely off the list. She was sure of it.

She pulled into a parking spot at the church and got out.

Put on a smile. You need to inspire the cast.

Help me, God. Please help me. I need to remain calm and encouraging. I need to have faith in my students and not be so preoccupied with my own worries about my mother. I need to believe You are watching over all of us and most important—Thy will be done. Amen

She got out of her car, tried to stand tall, hurried into the church and walked into the room with a forced smile on her face.

The first person she saw was Jade.

It looked like she'd been standing there waiting for her. She was pale, with dark circles underlining eyes glittered with tears.

"I'm so sorry, Ms. Davis," she said softly.

"Hey, Jade. Please don't worry. It's not your fault at all."

Serena looked around at the other students standing nearby. The whole cast looked horror-stricken, terrified, and close to tears as well.

She had to rally them.

"C'mon everyone. This is our last rehearsal. Let's give it our best." Serena attempted to sound positive and upbeat.

"But it's ruined," Julie said. "Everything's ruined."

"Why is that?"

"Jade's dad won't let her sing." Jacob threw up his arms in despair.

"It's okay." She watched Jade hang her head. "It's okay, everyone. Mr. Jenkins has his reasons. But please don't forget that we've worked hard and we'll make it work. God won't let us down now. So, who wants to lead us in prayer?"

"I will," Jade said.

Serena was surprised. "Okay, go ahead."

"Can we all hold hands?" she asked.

"Yeah, let's." Jacob reached out to take Jade's.

They all gathered together, forming one complete circle. Serena looked around. In many ways it was quite sweet seeing donkeys and sheep, angels and the Holy Family all united, but the glum faces were unnerving.

"Dear God," Jade prayed. "I'm sorry I can't sing for You. I wanted to, but my dad is scared something might happen to me like it did to my mom. Please forgive him for not trusting in You." Serena watched her look around at all her friends. "You know, my mom always saw the good in everyone and everything. She could see something positive all the time. She'd point out a rainbow in stormy weather, a comforting hug when someone was sad and her smile could light up the world. Please, God, help us to be like her. Help us to remember that this is all about the birth of Jesus and try to be the best we can. If we do our part, we can trust that You'll do Your part too, God. Amen."

Sweet, honest and powerful.

Serena sensed a collective sigh of relief at Jade's words. Somehow, they had adopted the girl as their leader and she inspired them to keep going. Thank goodness. Jade's pep talk was just what they needed.

"Let's do this," Jacob said, sounding pumped.

"Yes, let's try hard," added Julie.

And so it began...

A complete dress rehearsal.

Oh, sure there were the standard mishaps.

Mary tripped as usual, a donkey trotted off in the wrong direction, one of the angels almost toppled off her perch, Joseph just about dropped the doll and fell trying to catch it, but all in all, it went pretty well.

There was even a bit more spark today, probably due to Jade's words, but it was still far from perfect by a long shot. At least they were focused and not continually whispering and chatting. It had driven her crazy these past few weeks when for some reason they all seemed concerned about other things and were talking up a storm behind her back. Then they'd quiet down when she came near them. Probably wondering what gifts they'd get on Christmas Day, was her guess.

Everyone looked her way when it was finished.

She clapped with enthusiasm.

"Good job. And that's a wrap. Please gather around."

"It wasn't any good," Julie said, looking frustrated.

"Sure it was," a voice from the back said.

They all turned.

"Oh, hi Sunny. Surprised to see you here. Everyone, this is Sunny. Most of you have probably seen her at Petals. She volunteers there."

She carried a large box.

"Sure do, and your mother sent me over with goodies. I got here early and I watched your rehearsal. It looked fantastic to me."

Bless Sunny for her positive input as she noticed the students perk up. She definitely lived up to her name.

"It really did?" asked Jacob.

"Yes, it did. Besides, rehearsals aren't supposed to be perfect, you know. You save all that positive energy for the actual performance."

"Well..." Julie giggled. "None of our practices have been perfect ever, so we should have the best pageant in the history of Angel on opening night."

That sure got a laugh out of all of them.

"Thanks, Sunny." Serena winked.

"So what's in the box?" asked Jacob.

"Cupcakes. Lots and lots of cupcakes."

Serena thought once again how her mother truly was a saint. This was exactly what they needed.

"Before we eat, can we pray again?" asked Julie.

"Certainly," Serena said, thrilled to see it was her students who were taking the initiative.

"Can I lead?" Julie asked.

"Go ahead."

"Okay, everyone hold hands and close your eyes."

Pause.

"Dear God, we pray that you will help us do our best tomorrow night. We pray for Jade so she is not too sad. We pray for her dad, too. And we also pray for Petals that somehow it will stay open. Amen."

How kind that they prayed for Jade, as well as Matt. And also for her mother's café.

Petals.

Serena felt a tear surface.

She couldn't even begin to fathom that it would be closing soon.

Don't think about that now.

She walked over to get a cupcake. A treat was just what she needed as well. Watching her students gulp down all the sweets in practically two bites, she reminded herself to thank her mother. Now the students would be leaving with smiles and icing on their happy faces.

It also gave her hope.

Surely a woman as kind as her mother wouldn't be left in the lurch.

Surely she could find a way to make Petals work and if not, God must have other plans for her.

Greater ones.

They just didn't know what they were, yet.

Twenty-seven

Matt pulled to a stop in front of the church.

Earlier he had dropped Jade off at school. As she turned to say goodbye, her sad eyes said it all and it hurt like anything to witness her pain.

They'd had plenty of talks about the reasoning behind his decision, but they ended up having to agree to disagree. She wanted to sing; he wanted to protect her. Her sadness touched his heart and snapped it in two. Dramatic? Yes. But it was how he felt.

Upset, restless, he had driven aimlessly around town, not sure what to do and somehow, he had landed here. At a church, of all places. He'd read in the bulletin on Sunday that it was left open all day for people looking to pray or just a quiet place to think. He also knew the pastor was at a food bank and busy, because he had seen him go in when he cruised down the main street. Maybe this was the very place he needed to find peace. To gather his thoughts. To calm his tired brain.

Sure, it was strange turning to a church.

At least, for him.

He was that desperate.

Hurrying out of his car, he ran up the steps to the front door, moving fast in case he backed out. Opening it, he quickly looked around. No one was there, so he walked to the front.

Kneeling, he was once again mesmerized by the candles and the large mural of Jesus painted across the front. The one in the hall chapel was of Jesus holding a lamb. This one showed a smiling Jesus talking to young children. He'd never noticed it on Sundays. Guess it was because his eyes usually never left Jade singing in the choir. Or Serena.

Once again, the compassion in the painting warmed Matt's heart. The pounding beats slowed, and he closed his eyes.

"Okay, God," he whispered. "I need help. I thought I did what You wanted by allowing Jade to sing. But now I'm so full of fear. I just can't let her go through with it, even if it's for a pageant about Your birth. I don't expect You to understand. Why should You? After all, I haven't been in good spirits in a long, long time."

A tear trickled down his cheek and he wiped it away. He didn't have time to cry. He needed answers.

"Honestly, I'm in a real mess. I'm so worried about losing Jade, and I ended up almost losing her anyway, because she ran away. She's still angry with me."

Exhausted, he rubbed his eyes and shook his head, trying to clear it.

"Not only that, I also told Serena off and she's been nothing but good to me and my daughter. She didn't deserve that."

Pause. His head spun.

"But it's mostly Jade I'm worried about."

Immediately, he felt the fear he had experienced the other night, when he couldn't find her, then discovered her safe at Petals.

"To be even more truthful, I wish my daughter didn't have a good singing voice. I know it's a gift, but I am afraid she will meet the same fate as my wife. When I was in the chapel the day we built the set, I felt it was the right decision to allow her to sing. But now I feel it's so wrong. Please let me know what to do. And also, how I can make peace with Jade and Serena."

He rested his head down on his arms.

Silence enveloped him.

He was tired. Just so tired...

"Are you okay there, Matt?"

Startled, his eyes opened.

Had he fallen asleep? He glanced at his watch. Fifteen minutes... he'd dozed off.

He knew he'd been up all night, so it shouldn't surprise him. But in a church?

And who was talking to him?

"Oh, hello Pastor Smythe."

"Hello, there. Are you all right?"

"Sure I am. Just tired."

"Sorry to disturb you, but I called your name several times and when you didn't answer, I got worried. You look upset."

"Guess I am." After all, he couldn't very well lie to a pastor.

"Do you want to talk about it?"

"No. It's okay."

"Well, you're in a church, so I figure it's something serious."

Their eyes locked.

The pastor's kindness won Matt over.

Before he knew it, he had broken down and told him everything. About Maya, about Jade, Serena, and Petals.

"What should I do, Reverend?"

The minister sat down beside him and said nothing. Silence reigned until after a minute or two he said softly, "God forgives you, my friend, but you need to forgive yourself for Maya's death. Seems to me you blame yourself, and in truth, you didn't cause it."

"But I could have prevented it."

"Do you think so, Matt? You hired a professional bodyguard and he got duped. You did what you could to protect her. You tried hard."

"I did, but it didn't work, and now I am so afraid of losing Jade."

"Yes, you are and rightly so. You are her father, her protector, and you want to keep her safe."

"But as my daughter points out," Matt said. "She has a gift she believes is from God. And she wants to serve God with her voice. So, what do I do? What is the right answer to all of this? I thought I knew, but now I don't." He paused again, feeling so much confusion circling around his head. "You know, when we were kids, we just used to sometimes ask ourselves what Jesus would do in certain circumstances. So, Reverend, just what would Jesus do here?"

The pastor was quiet again for a few minutes. Matt thought he might have fallen asleep because his eyes were closed, until suddenly they popped open and he said, "Well, one thing Jesus said was, *Therefore I tell you, do not worry about your life, what you will eat or drink; or about your body, what you will wear.*"

"But that's all I'm doing is worrying. I am filled with fear every minute of every day." Matt rubbed his eyes. "But I get what you're saying. You mean, I should trust God. Let go. But that's so hard to do."

"Yes, it is. It's a leap of faith. But somehow I believe you're ready for that jump." He smiled. "After all, you're here, and I've seen you at church the last couple of weeks."

"But just how do I take this leap? How do I let my daughter do something that might harm her?" He raised his eyes to the painting of Jesus. "But I guess forbidding her is harming her, too."

"You will find the way, Matt. I believe so. Your love for Jade will lead you."

Just like his daughter had been leading her friends in the pageant and also creating Angel Heart Gifts.

She was wiser than he was at any given moment.

"And now I have to leave you," the pastor said. "Sorry, I have an appointment, but please feel free to come and talk to me anytime."

"Thank you, Reverend."

"You'll figure this out, Matt. I know you will. Just trust, even a little."

With that, he left.

Matt closed his eyes again.

"Dear God, help me. I am afraid and only You can pull me out of it and show me the path I need to take."

He needed to believe. To have faith.

Could he?

Would he?

He wasn't sure.

O Holy Night...

Are you kidding me, he thought.

Was someone, somewhere, singing "O Holy Night?"

Was this a joke?

He looked around the church.

No one was there.

The stars are brightly shining...

He stood and hurried to the back of the church.

Nothing.

It is the night of the dear Savior's birth...

Was it coming from downstairs?

Was there a practice he didn't know of?

He glanced at his watch. It was twelve noon.

Long live the world in sin and error pining...

It had to be coming from below.

He ran down the stairs, taking them two at a time.

Opening the door slowly, he slid into the room.

Til he appeared and the soul felt its worth...

And there was Jade.

Eyes closed, darkness surrounding her, illuminated by a candle she was holding, singing her heart out.

He forgot she'd mentioned she'd been practicing using a microphone during lunch hour.

He just stood there watching her. Listening to her. So moved, his heart exploded with love.

He sank to his knees as the last few words of the song rang out.

O night divine...

Footsteps drew near.

"Dad? Dad? Is that you? Are you okay?"

"I'm fine, honey."

She leaned down to help him up and he hugged her tightly. Her arms wrapped around him, just as tight.

"Sorry, Dad. Sorry for singing. I just popped over here for a few minutes. Please, don't be mad."

He pulled back and stared into her eyes.

The pastor was right.

His love for his daughter showed him the way.

Twenty-eight

It was the night of the pageant.

Serena peeked out of the curtains and saw that every seat was filled. She took note of where her mother, Helen and Sunny were sitting, and right beside them were Nancy and Nick. Guess they were reconnecting, although her friend had remained quiet about it. Then again, they'd both been too busy to chat much.

Principal Lemire had been right all along.

Not that she thought he lied, but apparently there had never been such a large crowd. It had completely sold out and he'd even added extra seats, still complying with fire regulation codes, because when word got out that Jade was singing, everyone in town wanted to come.

Only one problem.

She wasn't singing.

Serena decided not to tell anyone, still hanging onto hope for a miracle.

Unfortunately, it was not to be.

Still, it was the largest turnout ever in Angel Elementary history.

Her heart raced.

Also on their side was the fact the predicted snowstorm, heralded by weather forecasters, had passed on by. Instead, they were left with a confection of large snowflakes softly drifting down, adding beautifully to the ambience. It also meant traveling was easy, as well as enchanted.

Too bad they'd all be disappointed.

Everyone was there but two people.

Matt.

And Jade.

Were they not coming? She'd assumed the girl would still take part in the pageant, just not sing.

She wondered if they'd stayed at home mourning Maya.

Sigh.

Maybe that was exactly what they needed to do. With a bit of shuffling, Serena could cover Jade's absence as one of the angels who led the procession. No one would know.

Except her heart.

Suffering Matt's wrath toward her still hurt.

Forget about that. Stay focused.

She glanced at her watch. Time to get moving.

Serena walked over to where she'd hung up her coat and picked up the red roses that were lying on a table. She had already made sure all her students were dressed and ready, and had quickly hurried out to the car to get the flowers. She registered she was nervous. Terrified, to be even more honest. She paused and stared up into the heavens.

Dear God, I have no singer and Principal Lemire will probably fire me on the spot, but I'm asking You to please bless this re-enactment. Bless all my students, who have worked so hard to pull this together. I deeply apologize for not trusting You and for being more worried about Petals' future than this pageant, but please guide us to be the best we can be. Help us to spread Your love and the joy of the real meaning of Christmas to everyone here. Happy Birthday, Jesus. This night belongs to you. Amen.

She finally felt she had her head on right for a change and was focused. And now she had to be strong for her students and hopefully—God-willing—be inspiring.

Taking a deep breath and letting it out slowly, she walked into the room they were holed up in.

"Look, Miss Davis, look." Jacob raised his arms. "I'm holding Christopher, I mean, the baby Jesus. Me and him are bonding big-time."

He looked so proud.

"Yes, you are. Good for you. You are doing a great job. I never doubted you one bit."

"Sure you did." He grinned, gently rocking the child.

She grinned back. "Well, occasionally I did."

"Yeah, but told you I could do it."

"Yes, you did."

"What are the roses for?" asked Julie, putting her phone down from what looked like a heated conversation. Her eyes kept darting to the door.

"You'll see. Are you okay? You look worried."

"No, no, I'm fine. But the flowers are beautiful. Did someone send them to you? For opening night?"

"No, I bought them. They are for each one of you. Now let's gather together."

Curious, they quickly formed a circle around her. She noticed Jade still wasn't there. Somehow, she'd hoped she had slipped in unnoticed and was going to make it after all.

Really, though?

Matt was not even going to let her show up for the pageant?

He must still be angry with her. Or, as she'd thought earlier, needed to be alone. Or both. But she sure wished they'd arrive. Jade had been such an important part of the pageant.

She shook her head, figuratively tossing away her concerns. She had an excited group of eager faces she needed to tend to. Besides, maybe he had taken his daughter on a vacation to get away from everything. To visit his sister, or something. She had to face the fact that, for whatever reason, they were skipping the re-enactment.

Well, here goes. Time to begin. She looked around at all their excited faces.

"My mother loves roses and whenever I was in a ballet recital, she gave me one for good luck before every single performance. She always thanked me for all my hard work, told me I had struggled like the stem of a rose through all the thorns and it was now time to bloom. I loved that she did that; it touched my heart and gave me courage, so tonight I am following in her tradition. I am giving each one of you a rose, from my heart to yours and I wish you all the best. You have all worked so hard and tonight is your night to shine for the glory of God. It is your time to blossom. Each one of you."

Surprisingly, they all clapped.

"Thank you," Jacob said. "And I'm sorry for all the times I acted silly in rehearsal."

"That's okay." Serena smiled reassuringly. "You stuck it out and you're doing well now. I'm proud of you."

"Thanks." Jacob smiled back.

"I'm nervous," Julie said. "Will we do okay? Did we practice enough?"

"We sure did," Serena said. "And you'll do just fine. Trust me, but most of all, trust God."

Once again, she raised her eyes to the heavens and sent out a silent prayer.

Please, Lord. Please help calm their nerves so they will do well, in Your honor.

She handed a rose to each one of them, witnessing up close their smiles, their happiness, even a sense of peace at what they were doing.

They were ready. Definitely. As ready as could be.

"Now who will lead us with a prayer before we go on?" she asked.

Jacob raised his hand.

"I will. I will."

"Hurry," Julie called out. "We begin in about five minutes."

It was also about the tenth time she had looked at her phone. Serena wondered what that was all about. Did it concern her parents? Were they late or something?

"I'll hurry," Jacob said, sitting, holding little Christopher who was remarkably still asleep. He said softly, "Dear Lord. Today we honor the birth of the baby Jesus. May we do Him proud. Amen. Oh, and please take care of Jade, wherever she is."

Serena smiled. Short and sweet, but just right. And his concern for his friend was very touching.

"Now, go on out and just be the best you can be," Serena said. "I'm so proud of each and every one of you. Oh, and please don't forget to enjoy it. Remember, if you make a mistake, don't let on and no one will know. Just keep on going."

Hugs ensued and Serena grabbed the opportunity to whisper in Julie's ear, "Are you okay? I've noticed you keep looking at your phone."

To her surprise, the girl blushed.

"Yeah, yeah, I'm fine."

"Okay, then."

Whatever it was, Julie kept it to herself.

Because the procession began at the back of the hall, Serena led the group down a long hallway, out of sight, and lined them up in the entryway. She waved to Principal Lemire to give him the agreed upon cue that they were ready. He walked to the microphone, introduced the pageant with a prayer and it was time to begin. Serena still hadn't told him she had no singer, but figured he'd find out soon enough. She hadn't wanted to deal with his frustration and possible lectures, needing to keep upbeat for her students, since they were performing, no matter what.

She sucked in her breath again and slowly let it out.

Breathe. In and out. In and out.

It was time.

She whispered to the first angel to begin the trek down the aisle. Slowly they walked, their candles glowing brightly, beacons of hope, peace and love.

The audience hushed.

It was the beginning. Of what might mean the end, for her.

Dear God. Everything is in your hands. Please bless my class.

This prayer was her mantra tonight.

She so wanted her students to do well.

Moving to a side aisle, she leaned up against the wall, pulling her dad's plaid shirt tightly around her. Yes, she'd worn it, hoping its warmth and comfort would help her find strength tonight. Heart pounding, she watched their every step, every move, every word.

And the play went well.

Surprisingly well.

Over the top well.

She shouldn't have been so surprised, after all the practicing they did, but she was.

It truly was amazing.

The innkeeper remembered his words, Mary and Joseph took turns holding the baby, which seemed to touch the hearts of many. Jacob handled little Christopher like a pro...thank goodness he had not dropped him even once, and pride oozed from him. He was certainly not the class clown tonight and even Julie seemed to forgive him, judging by her smiles.

All angels, donkeys and sheep performed well.

No one tripped or fell or messed up their lines.

An absolute Godsend.

Now it was time for the meditation and the song.

The not so great part.

Serena's heart sank as she walked to the podium, noticing how happy Principal Lemire looked, sporting a huge smile. Unfortunately, she'd be wiping it off his face soon when she played the musical tape. He was sure to be disappointed.

Back to the present.

Serena's job was to introduce Julie, who was delivering the meditation. The group had held many discussions about this and she had been elected. Serena reached for the notes in her pocket but became alarmed the closer she moved towards the stage.

What was wrong with Julie?

She looked terrified. Again. Not only that, she kept staring at Serena.

Was she sick? Too frightened to continue?

Was that it?

She knew Julie had written her speech, so maybe someone else could read it. Jacob, maybe?

Her mind spinning, Serena continued to the podium. Suddenly the door at the back opened. Gasps of surprise rang out, and, noticing Julie's grimace change into a huge smile, she turned to look.

What was going on?

To her shock, down the center aisle walked Jade. Dressed as an angel. Standing at the door behind her was Matt, looking nervous.

Jade walked towards Serena holding a yellow rose. It was obviously planned ahead of time because she had once mentioned she loved yellow roses. The girl winked as she handed Serena the rose, whispering, "This is for you. Trust us, please."

Serena smiled, realizing something was happening and she had no clue what it could be. So, she took hold of the microphone and carried on with her planned introduction. She thanked everyone for attending, made a few comments about how hard the class had worked, then handed the microphone to Julie, who still couldn't stop grinning. Serena nodded at Jade as she walked back down to claim her place back against the wall, curious over the statement about trust. What was she to trust in?

"Hello, everyone," Julie said. She waited a second while everyone said 'hello' back.

"We have a big surprise for Ms. Davis."

To Serena's shock, everyone smiled and nodded as if they were all in on it.

Her mind spun. What had these children planned?

"She thinks I am saying the meditation," continued Julie. "Instead, the class secretly chose Jade Jenkins."

What? Serena was indeed shocked. Was that what all that continuous whispering in class had been all about? And why Julie seemed alarmed earlier? She looked over at Jade, whose smile was so wide, it literally took Serena's breath away. She had never seen her look so happy as she took hold of the microphone. She literally glowed, or blazed, was more like it.

"Thank you," Jade said. "Thank you for the honor of writing a meditation about the Christmas story." She paused, suddenly looking nervous, and Serena noticed that Julie took hold of one hand and Jacob stood on her other side, still holding little Christopher, for support. Jade smiled and mouthed 'thank you.'

How beautiful to be able to witness this, thought Serena. A total rose petal moment of blossoming after traveling through the thorns.

"Saint John said," Jade continued, "for God so loved the world that He gave His one and only Son, that whoever believes in Him shall not perish, but have eternal life." She paused for a moment to let the words sink in, then began to speak. "This is what Christmas is all about. So let us all close our eyes and reflect on that very first Christmas many years ago. It was a lot like what we saw tonight. It was all about love. The love that shone from Mary and Joseph's eyes was all that the baby Jesus needed. It was a night that changed the world forever. God's love, shining through Jesus, showed us how to care for others, how to listen, and how to help each other. May we always remember to keep the Christmas love story with us every single day of our lives."

She then burst into "O Holy Night."

Serena's eyes popped open as tears welled in her eyes at how beautifully this young girl sang. She looked around and could visibly see how Jade's message, through words and song, seemed to touch a chord with every single person. There were smiles, tears, and joyful expressions. It was truly spectacular and moving.

Someone came up beside her.

"Are you okay?" She turned to find Matt there, looking concerned.

"Yes." She touched his arm. "You let her sing. Thank you."

"But you're crying."

"Tears of joy."

He smiled. "As you always reminded me, I need to let her light shine. For God."

"Are *you* okay?"

"Yes, I'm finally okay."

Serena noticed how, for the first time since they had reconnected, he looked at peace. To her surprise, more tears flowed at this brave man who had finally conquered his fear. And to shock her more, his arm wrapped around her shoulders. She leaned closer, craving his warmth during such an emotional time.

At the end of the song, Julie said, "We also have another surprise."

Serena gasped. What other surprise could there possibly be?

"As you all know," Julie continued. "We have a tradition here at Angel, to give donations collected tonight to help someone. Well, Ms. Davis, we are doing things slightly different. We kept who we were helping secret from you."

What? thought Serena. What were they talking about?

"You may have noticed a lot of whispering during rehearsal times," Jacob said.

Serena nodded. She sure did, always struggling to keep them focused.

"We apologize to you, but it was just that we had a lot to discuss. So, here's our secret." He grinned. "Inspired by Jade's mom, we, Ms. Davis' seventh grade class, agreed to take part in Angel Heart gifts. We also convinced the whole town to join in. The goal was to find someone who needed help and to reach out to assist them. We all knew who we wanted to help and we have been doing something in private for someone, totally behind our teacher's back."

Serena was confused.

What did he mean? The money gathered tonight was to go to the church to sponsor free dinners for those in need. They had all agreed upon that.

Jacob continued, "Quietly and without Ms. Davis knowing, we have been secretly collecting money for over a month, doing all sorts of things."

"Some of us have saved our babysitting money, sold baked goods, helped people shovel driveways and worked extra for any money we could get," added Julie. "We also had a lot of donations from every business in town and from lots of benefactors."

"Speaking of benefactors, we have someone special here tonight." Jade winked at Serena. "We now ask Mr. Anderson to come up. And also Mrs. Davis."

What? Her mother? And Mr. Anderson? The owner of the building housing the bakery? But he lived down south now. What was he doing there?

Her mom looked at her for some kind of clarification, but Serena just shrugged. She had no idea what was going on.

A smiling Mr. Anderson walked to the microphone. Serena had met him a few times over the years and she watched him warmly greet her mother who stood to his side, while Jade, Julie and Jacob stood on the other side.

Mr. Anderson began. "A little while ago, a young girl by the name of Jade Jenkins sent me an email." He smiled over at her and she beamed at him. "She wanted to talk to me about something. So, we set up a conference call with Jade, myself and her father. She had a project she thought I might be interested in. It was called Angel Heart Gifts."

Serena's mother looked surprised. So did Serena.

"That's why we were late," whispered Matt. "Sorry about that, but we had to pick Mr. Anderson up at the airport and the plane wasn't on time."

"You flew him up here?"

He grinned. "Yes, I did. We planned to be here earlier so Jade could tell you she could sing."

What?

"I was told that everything was to be done in secret," Mr. Anderson said, cutting into Serena's thoughts. "And it was, judging by the looks of surprise on Ms. Davis and her mother's faces. The students wanted to keep it quiet even from them, but we knew eventually they would have to know, although the process to get here was a secret."

Know what? thought Serena.

"This young lady," he gestured towards Jade, "came up with a strategy to save Petals."

Serena's heart flip-flopped so fast she thought she'd pass out. Her mother looked just as shocked, swayed a little, so Serena hurried over to wrap her arms around her.

"I must say," Mr. Anderson said. "I was quite impressed by Jade's strategizing, commitment, not to mention her well-worked-out plan."

Serena looked down at Matt, who smiled widely. He winked at her.

"It was a pleasure to work with these fine individuals," continued Mr. Anderson. "Jade's class got involved, and subsequently, as Jacob said, the whole town of Angel. I also know it is tradition at the pageant to announce where the money collected goes, so I now get the honor of telling you that the recipient this year of all the donations is Petals." He looked at Serena's mother. "We are pleased to tell you that your town, with the leadership of this seventh grade, produced enough money for a down payment for the building and the mortgage has been paid for the year. The building is yours, and Petals will live on."

He handed over what looked like the deed to the building.

Jade walked over to the microphone. "Mr. Anderson is forgetting to mention one thing." She smiled over at him. "He reduced the price of the building, which was his gift to all of us, and to Mrs. Davis."

Serena gasped.

How had she ever doubted God?

Sometimes help came to you in ways you'd least expect it. And never, ever, had she expected this.

She was speechless. So was her mother. Somehow, they managed to say thank you. Few words but tears of joy that spoke volumes.

As people piled out to gather at Petals for refreshments, already planned by her mother, Principal Lemire walked up to her. "That was the best pageant ever," he said. "And I have an early Christmas gift for you. I want you to know that, as of this moment, I'm hiring you full time."

Serena gasped.

"I have the job?"

"Yes. You deserve it."

"And you knew what my students were planning?"

"Certainly, they ran it by me. It was perfect and sure showed their love for you. Now, come on over to Petals so we can celebrate."

"Yes, sir. Be there in a few minutes."

As he walked away, Serena glanced up to the heavens.

Thank you, God.

It was all she had left to say.

As she and her mother personally thanked her grinning students she thought of the words of Jesus. *"I praise You, Father, Lord of heaven and earth, because You have hidden these things from the wise and learned, and revealed them to little children."*

She knew they weren't children, but they were certainly wise and learned, well beyond their years. They had, in fact, created a miracle.

She hugged her mother even tighter.

The bakery was saved.

God had blessed them in every way. Even provided a singer.

She should have trusted more, but was glad she persevered, even in the midst of fear and often hopelessness.

Thank you, God, she whispered once again. *Thank you, thank you, thank you.*

Twenty-nine

Petals was aglow.

Looked like the whole town of Angel had showed up to partake in hot chocolate and goodies.

Serena noticed how her mother shone, as the two of them joined Sunny and Helen to place platters of baked goods throughout the café. What was sweeter was that people were trying to pay for their treats and Mary wouldn't let them. Instead, they put their money in a large glass bowl someone had brought and placed on the counter, anticipating this. Such kind people lived in this town. Serena would never forget them.

She looked around.

There was so much love in this room, and her heart was full. She had never felt happier than she did at that very moment.

"We did okay, right?" asked Jacob, running over to see her, blue icing smeared across his cheek from the cupcake he was eating.

"You did way more than okay," Serena said. "I just can't believe what all of you accomplished."

"We surprised you, didn't we?" Julie asked, joining the two of them.

"Yes, you did. I can never thank you enough."

"No need to thank us," said Jacob. "You put up with us through all those rehearsals."

"And you were terrific." Serena smiled.

"We're just glad the bakery will be saved," Julie said.

"Yeah, my birthday's coming up," Jacob added. "And I want your mom to bake my cake."

"Oh, I'm sure she'd be honored to do that." Serena stepped back to allow Helen to serve them from a platter of hot chocolate. They helped themselves to a steaming cup each.

"You see. It all worked out."

Serena turned to find Nancy behind her, grinning away.

"It did." She reached out to hug her friend. "I know you would have had a hand in all of this. Thanks for all your support."

"No problem."

Serena pulled away.

"And one day you'll have to tell me what's going on with you and Nick."

"Only if you let me know about you and Matt."

"I definitely think we need a good old gab session."

"Yes, we do. How about tomorrow we meet for a walk? A long one."

"I'll be there."

Watching Nancy head over to Nick, Serena noticed Jade standing off to one side.

She walked over to join her. "Your singing was so beautiful."

"It was?" Jade looked surprised.

No ego with this girl, that was a definite.

"Yes. And I can't believe you saved Petals, too. You were the one who planned it all out. The mastermind."

"Oh, it was the community support that made it all happen." Jade grinned. "But I'll let you in on a secret. I started planning it the day of my birthday. So who says birthday wishes don't come true? Because mine sure did."

"This was your birthday wish?"

"Yes. I knew it would make you happy."

"You're such an amazing person, Jade. So selfless and loving. Did you make peace with your dad, too?

"Yeah." She nodded vigorously. "Guess he's okay, after all. He finally came to his senses and let me sing."

"He sure did."

But what was he doing?

As Jade scampered off to join her friends, she noticed Matt off in the corner by himself holding a large shopping bag. She hurried over to the counter and hid behind a pillar to watch him.

He walked to the back of the room, suddenly stopped, and pulled something out of the bag.

Looking around, making sure no one saw him, not aware she was secretly observing him, he placed a gold nutcracker amid all the other ones. He then crumpled the bag and pretended to nonchalantly walk to where the cookie platters were

"Like daughter, like father," Serena said, joining him.

He looked shocked.

"What do you mean? I don't sing. Or dance."

"But you're kind. Now what was that all about?" She pointed to the gold nutcracker.

"You saw me do that?"

"I did."

He smiled. "You weren't supposed to. It was my Heart Gift, to be done in secret."

"Figured so."

"Guess it wasn't so secret."

Serena leaned over and whispered, "You knew my mother sold it?"

"Yes. I heard her say so the night you had your class here."

"But how did you manage to find it?" She glanced over at the nutcracker, marveling at its beauty.

"Oh, I have my ways. I managed to trace it down and bought it back." He winked. "With the help of Helen."

Could she get any happier? Yes, she could. She reached out to squeeze his hand.

"Wow. Thank you. My mother will be thrilled. She loved that nutcracker."

He stared at her hand, clasping it tighter. "But you can't let on I put it there."

"Okay, I won't." She pulled her hand away, embarrassed that she'd grabbed it in the first place. "Thank you for all your help with saving Petals. You have quite the daughter, you know."

"That I do."

"And you were in on her plans?"

"Yes." He chuckled. "She even asked if she could hire me as her lawyer, *pro bono* of course, to draw up the papers to purchase this building."

"I think you might have a lawyer on your hands."

"Or a singer."

"Are you okay with that?"

"Yes. And I'm sorry I was so rude to you the other night. I jumped to conclusions and I should never have done that."

"Well, I won't lie. I was hurt, but I do understand. After all, I did the same to you back in seventh grade."

He paused, just staring at her. She stared right on back.

"Do you understand enough to let me ask you out on an actual date?" he asked.

"Yes."

A hug never felt so good.

And that kiss...

Meet Suzanne M Hurley

Happiness to this author, is being curled up with her laptop, creating imaginary worlds that come from her heart. Writing is her passion and dreaming up story lines is her love.

Suzanne was born in Peterborough, Ontario and currently resides in Caledonia, Haldimand County, where on morning walks with Rico, she tries out her new plots on the cows, sheep and numerous wild animals she greets along the way.

You can visit Suzanne M Hurley at her website: http:// suzannemhurley.blogspot.ca/

Other Works From The Pen Of

Suzanne M Hurley

Samantha Barclay Mystery Series:

Changeable Facades - A murder has been committed! No one believes it but a young boy and his high school counselor. Will they catch the killers before he or she strikes again?

Delusions - Narcotics are sweeping Milton High! A student is dead! Lies and Deceit take over, as high school counselor Samantha Barclay is immersed in yet another deadly drama.

Chances – FBI Agent Ryan Leam's son is missing. Psychologist Samantha Barclay risks her life to go undercover at Sacred Heart Academy, seeking truth. The results are shocking and unbelievable.

Shades of Envy – Dead bodies are stacking up! Teenagers want to be vampires! The sheriff is acting secretively! Psychologist Samantha Barclay sets out on a wild ride to uncover the truth. Her discoveries lead to confrontations of the deadly kind. Will she survive with her life, as well as her heart intact?

Who did it? – Who killed the beloved principal of St. Michael's High School? Newly minted FBI agent Samantha Barclay's first case is to find the murderer. Only one problem. Everyone she meets has a reason to see him dead. Will she uncover who did it – before he or she strikes again?

Love? – Samantha Barclay discovers what people will do in the name of love, when a dead body is discovered in her basement and her beloved step-mother is arrested for murder.

Guilt – Who killed Doctor Ingrid Sayers? High school teacher David Harris says he did. Samantha Barclay disagrees and races against all odds to find the real murderer

The Cookie Club – One by one, the residents of Landon, West Virginia, are dropping dead. FBI/school psychologist Samantha Barclay, sets out to find the killer, before it becomes a ghost town.

Women's Fiction:

Nice Girls Can Win – Lawyer Jessie White is fired, evicted and jilted, all on the same day. Hitting rock bottom, she moves back home and immediately ends up in a sparring match with 'Red', the hunky guy next door. She soon discovers that miracles really do happen and how love often finds you, just when you're not looking.

Wings of the Past – Zoey Avery thinks she is happy, until wedding thoughts infiltrate her marriage-phobic mind. Only one problem – the groom she is dreaming about is a man she hasn't seen in thirteen years.

The Dream Smasher – Best-selling author Tracy Hazel is devastated to discover she is the victim of identify theft, when someone submits a horrid book, claiming she wrote it.

The Christmas Rose – Sparks fly, when Principal Olivia Lyons tries to uncover which student stole a million-dollar Christmas ornament. Her new guidance head thinks she did it. Will she end up in jail, love, or both?

Always Love– Jenna Evans has no idea she is in a coma. She believes she has somehow landed in a fantasy world where everyone is supportive and lives in peace. Will she return to her husband and children? It all comes down to love - real love. What will she choose?

Young Adult

The Teddy Bear Eye Club – Depressed, fourteen-year-old Mayah Lewis hides from the world, until she befriends new girl, beautiful bald-headed Celeste Daniels. Everything begins looking up, until one day, Celeste disappears.

Letter to Our Readers

Enjoy this book?

You can make a difference.

As an independent publisher, Wings ePress, Inc. does not have the financial clout of the large New York publishers. We can't afford large magazine spreads or subway posters to tell people about our quality books.

But we do have something much more effective and powerful than ads. We have a large base of loyal readers.

Honest reviews help bring the attention of new readers to our books.

If you enjoyed this book, we would appreciate it if you would spend a few minutes posting a review on the site where you purchased this book or on the Wings ePress, Inc. webpages at: https://wingsepress.com/

Thank You

Visit Our Website

For The Full Inventory
Of Quality Books:

Wings ePress.Inc
https://wingsepress.com/

Quality trade paperbacks and downloads
in multiple formats,
in genres ranging from light romantic comedy
to general fiction and horror.
Wings has something for every reader's taste.
Visit the website, then bookmark it.
We add new titles each month!

Wings ePress Inc.
3000 N. Rock Road
Newton, KS   67114